A FOREST ENCOUNTER

A murder occurs in a National Park in West Virginia. Two women from very different backgrounds are brought together and form an emotional bond as they strive to manage the tragedy. While the ideal of justice being served is a compelling motivator, each woman faces the test of courage to move forward in her own life. Both must confront their isolation and the fear of risking love.

The author weaves timeless themes of class struggle, emotional loss, and recovery.

AMAZON-VERIFIED REVIEWS

Praise For Deborah Donaldson's First Novel,

SECOND CHANCES

2024 NEXT GENERATION INDIE BOOK AWARD FINALIST

"It takes a pretty good book to keep me engaged and Second Chances hit the mark. Each chapter kept me wanting more. Definitely give Second Chances a read!!"

"I love the way this author writes. She gives such amazing detail without boring or making the reader think, 'let's get on with it.' The characters are marvelous. The story is sexy, smart, and addictive. I cannot wait for the second book to be published."

"The skilled combination of romance and mystery made for an exciting read in and of itself, but the author's background in psychology brings a depth and character development that's hard to find in books of this genre. Highly recommend!"

"Second Chances combines all of my favorite things – mystery, murder, romance, intrigue, and lots of plot twists and turns. It's a pager-turner of the finest order. I can't wait to see what Ms. Donaldson comes up with in her next book."

"This book brought me back to my college years as an athlete and navigating my journey of self-discovery. Relatable to everyone who had a star-crossed relationship! I enjoyed the mystery which kept the story moving, A fun read! Looking forward to the next book from this author."

Published by Bardolf & Company

A Forest Encounter
A Mystery Romance

ISBN 978-1-938842-82-5

For information:
Bardolf & Company
www.bardolfandcompany.com
941-232-0113

Cover design & layout by:
Parker Pad & Printing Ltd.
www.parkerpad.com

ACKNOWLEDGMENTS

Early in my adult life I visited Canyon de Chelly. It is located in the Navajo Reservation in Arizona. It has been inhabited continuously for nearly 5,000 years and is the only National Monument owned by the Navajo nation.

On that first trip I went with the required Navajo guide and was allowed to approach Spider Rock from the valley floor. I walked in the valley next to Chinle creek which splits and curves around the base of the two spires that rise 750 feet above the junction of Canyon de Chelly and Monument Canyon. The red sandstone spires rising out of the bright green canyon floors literally took my breath away. And I felt an immense feeling of awe and an overwhelming spirit of holiness. The Navajo believe that their ancestors emerged from living under ground to their above ground existence here at Spider Rock.

When I visited two years ago, the drought had taken its toll on the vegetation and tourists were no longer allowed to approach the spires from where I had stood years before. The gift of my recent visit was being led on a hike by a Navajo Park Service employee, Casey Teseny, who made the personal stories of the drawings on the rock walls come alive. He also shared stories of his people and their culture. His reverence for his ancestors and this land convinced me that I wanted to write a novel that borrowed on the rich history of his people.

So, I started my research on the Navajo history and culture

and beliefs. I highly recommend Jim Kristofics epic book, *Medicine Women*, a fascinating account of the trading post that became a settlement, and then the Presbyterian Church-assisted mission that established the first Native American Nursing School established in Ganado. I also want to recommend James McNeley's *Holy Wind in Navajo Philosophy.* His book was an invaluable source for understanding the Navajo concept of personality.

The second major source of inspiration for this novel came from Peggy Orser, a friend who shared her stories of growing up in West Virginia and who was able to overcome her small-town background to have a life of international travel and accomplishment in the Federal Government. Both Casey and Peggy spoke of the courage of mothers and grandmothers and that motif resonates with my own background.

Primary readers help authors who self-publish turn the corner on confidence and often add astute suggestion about plot and tempo. Thank you, Jacqueline Fein-Zachary. Besides being a published author yourself (*Harvest Host*) you could easily hire out as an editor. Your eye for detail and themes is remarkable.

I want to thank my sister, Tina. Your suggestions for this book made it better and your love for me helps me feel safer on this planet.

The last major source of inspiration were the staff and students at Berea College, located in Berea, Kentucky. Berea was the first integrated co-educational college in the South. It is a tuition free school that requires all the students to contribute to their education by working at the school, and it has a very high rate of their graduates passing their licensing exams in teaching and nursing. Thank you, Dr. Sue Raimondo, director of counseling services, for your time in meeting with me and giving me the actual feeling of the skill and compassion, you bring to helping the students who need your services. Thank you, Brendan Nichols, for giving me a detailed architectural tour of the campus and its rich cultural history.

Thank you, Marianne Harvey. You did such a good job of formatting my book and helping me with various grammar dilemmas. Your judgement about the visual layout of text and the decisions you made for the layout of the cover were very helpful. And you are one of the fastest processors I have ever met.

Thank you Chris Angermann, editor extraordinaire. The suggestions you made after only a brief read of my initial manuscript were spot on.

Thank you, Janis Parker, for helping me to get my book formatted and printed in an economical way. Your generosity and kindness is a gift to all who know you.

While *A Forest Encounter* is a work of fiction I hope it showcases two causes that are worthy of other people's support. I had thought of donating 50% of all book sales to Berea and a Navajo charity. However, books that are self-published, can often earn a return of $300.00 or so a year (after the expense of Amazon, printing, and shipping). Writing a book that is self-published is kind of an expensive hobby. So, it seems specious of me to declare that I am sharing my book sales. If you are moved to help Berea continue in its mission, or if you wish to donate to help services for children on the Navajo reservation, look below for credible nonprofit charities.

Futures For Children
9600 Tennyson Street, NE Albuquerque, NM 87122
505-821-2828

Berea College Donations
101 Chestnut Street, Berea, KY 40404
www.berea.edu

To my readers, thank you for the time you have taken to read my book. Please leave a review if you liked it and recommend it to your friends who read. My book is available in paperback, Kindle and audio.

A FOREST ENCOUNTER

a mystery romance

DEBORAH DONALDSON

Bardolf & Company
Sarasota, Florida

CHAPTER 1

At 2 PM the last of the wilderness campers made their way to the counter. The wilderness campsites had no electricity or water spigots, but they were typically near a creek or pond. Campers had to carry all their gear in backpacks to their site. That would include pills or a filter to make the water safe, all their food, fuel for a camp stove for cooking, and tents for shelter.

The line wasn't too long this Saturday morning, Lona thought as she unlocked the door at the check-in center. Lona Johnson was a transfer from a national park in the West, and she felt like an outsider at this park in West Virginia. She had only been working here for six weeks, having helped get the park and the buildings ready for the summer crowds. It was still early in the spring, and she hoped to be able to finally get some time off to explore some of the more remote trails this weekend.

There were four in this last group. All appeared to be in their late teens or early twenties. *These people are clearly not the typical backpackers*, she thought, as she examined their T-shirts and shorts and tennis shoes. Their backpacks appeared to be stuffed with items appropriate for car camping, but way too much weight for comfortable backpacking. Two scruffy young men stood in front. The larger of the two was wearing camouflage shirt and pants. His clothes looked like official army clothing with a name tag on the shirt. The young man wearing them looked too young to be the original owner. The clothes were baggy and stained, but how can you tell with camo, she thought. Both young men had shaggy hair that needed cutting and cleaning. Neither of them had shaved in several days.

The other two could not have looked more different from the front guys. They wore clean, fitted, but comfortable clothes and could have walked off the campus of a college. The young woman had thick blond hair cut in a short and stylish manner, hanging just past her jaw. She wore no make-up, but her striking blue eyes certainly grabbed attention, nonetheless. She stared back at Lona's examination of her with a glare that only a young woman can pull off. Her companion (boyfriend?) was slender and didn't seem to have any facial hair. His jeans were almost too clean for a weekend in the woods. While the young woman was also slender, she seemed quite fit and her shorts revealed strong legs, while her T-shirt showcased well-developed arms. Lona wondered if she was a college-level athlete.

"You guys are getting sort of a late start for backpacking and for the weather that is forecast for tonight. We expect rain and possibly hail at the higher elevations. I hope you brought some cold-weather gear," she offered with as warm a tone as she could manage. She also gave a soft smile to the two who were standing to the side.

"Hey, Pocahontas, don't you worry about us. We can keep each other warm enough," said one of the scruffy ones.

Lona felt like ice water had been thrown in her face. Her smile quickly vanished. She addressed the boy with the sneer. *Was he actually licking his lips?* "You are correct that I am a descendant of the indigenous people of North America. Of course, Pocahontas was from the Powhatan tribe in coastal Virginia. I am a member of the Navajo tribe, further west of here. Can I please see your site registration and dates?"

"Hey, Babe, if you want to visit us tonight, just let me know and I'll leave a light on," said the young man who seemed to be the leader of the group.

Lona looked over at the couple on the side who appeared slightly embarrassed by their companion. Scruffy guy number two just looked bored. Lona turned to her colleague who had just come in from the back office and had heard the flirty invitation.

"Hey, Jim, do you mind finishing their check in? I have some data I need to get into the computer before we close today."

She turned and went into the back room, exchanging an eye roll with Jim as she slipped past him. *Thank goodness I pulled this shift with Jim.* Jim Schaeffer was a career national park service employee and looked every inch the part. At six feet tall, with salt and pepper hair, fit and relaxed body, he could be on the poster for recruiting park employees. Besides looking the part, he really knew the forest and the animals in this area and had been generous in teaching her. In only two months she had started what felt like a good professional relationship, and more importantly, the beginnings of a friendship with Jim.

She let herself enjoy the fantasy of jumping across the counter and pinning Mr. Scruffy beard to the wall with her forearm pressing his neck in a very uncomfortable way. She told herself as she departed, *No use getting a note in my file for sober and disorderly.*

As she left, Jim took down the registration and site numbers and looked at the names on the reservation. "Hmm, Preston Stuart, I see you were the one who obtained the reservation. You should bear in mind that Ranger Lona Johnson is a veteran of the armed services, honorably discharged from serving tours in Afghanistan. She deserves some respect."

Lona closed the door, not wanting to hear Preston's reply. *Breathe in, breathe out, picture the woods,* she told herself. She sat down and entered data into the computer. Ten minutes later Jim came into the back office and got himself a cup of coffee and offered one to Lona. She smiled her thanks.

"Lona, sometimes it embarrasses me to be in the same gender as that doofus," Jim said, sliding into the open chair in the office.

"Thank you for taking over for me. I could feel myself on the verge of using a tone that would create a bad review for the staff here." She looked up with a genuine smile. "Jim you make up for at least ten of them. I'm kind of worried though – that young woman, I don't know. I keep thinking of the tethered rabbits that are used to bait predators."

"Lona, I think your imagination is running a little too much in the wrong direction. She'll be in the tent with the boyfriend."

"Yeah, I know, but he didn't look like he could wrestle up two divisions. The other two have at least thirty pounds more body weight on them."

"Get some sleep, and then enjoy your days off. Are you packed?"

"I've been packed for two days. I think the front will blow out by noon tomorrow, but I want to get an early start, nonetheless. "

"Have a good time. Don't forget to leave your route on the desk in case anything goes wrong. We'll see you in four days?"

"Yep, I'll be opening up again on Tuesday morning."

Lona finished her work and let Jim lock up the building. Walking the half mile to the staff lodging, she kept replaying the encounter with the last group she checked in. She understood perfectly why she was uncomfortable with that guy, Preston. *Wow, what a piece of work he was. He and his buddy looked like they needed to be bathed and have their mouths washed out with soap.* She smiled at the memory of her mother once washing her mouth out with soap when she had cussed as a little girl.

But the other two, hair and clothes neat, it just didn't fit. She thought again of the image of rabbits as bait. *Hell, it'll be light for another few hours and I'm all packed, I'll get an early start on my trip. The campsite is on my way. I'll sleep better if I know she's okay.* She slung her backpack over her shoulder and locked the door behind her.

CHAPTER 2

Allie was making her way along the trail, and the boys were far enough ahead of her that she couldn't hear them. She walked along, lost in her thoughts, and keeping her eyes on the ground to avoid tripping over the tree roots. *What a way to spend spring break. I wish Matt hadn't arranged this trip with his cousin RJ, and that oaf, Preston. I don't know why Matt keeps trying to prove something to them. The time Matt and I have been away at college has really increased the gap between us.*

I wish it was just me and Matt on this trip. I wish he was here taking some of this weight off my back. She imagined him helping her and then smiled at the memory of Matt helping her when she was in second grade. The teacher had refused to respond to her desperate waving of her hand to request a bathroom break. Then Bobby Burkes yelled out to everyone in the class that she had peed at her desk. She could still feel the shame of that and the gratitude when Matt stayed by her side at recess and held her hand. He didn't leave her side, even on the walk home. He was with her, just being quiet. *Maybe Matt and I can find a way to have some time together and really talk about our lives.*

I don't think Preston has been a good influence on RJ.

I am beginning to wonder if they have gotten into the drug scene here. They deny it, but they seem so different from when we were all in high school. And I'm sick and tired of Preston teasing me about how college has made Matt and me "too big for our britches." I want to be able to enjoy these woods, but I wanted to puke when Preston talked to that pretty woman that way. Hmm, pretty?

She kept picturing the uniform and how it looked on the Ranger. She had thick dark hair pulled into a ponytail, dark, finely shaped eyebrows, and light brown skin. *Pretty? No, powerful. She must have been 5'9 or '10. So, a couple of inches taller than me. And she was very much in control. She certainly wasn't afraid of Preston as she corrected him on his Pocahontas tribe stuff. I liked how she just turned away and walked out of the room as if Preston wasn't worth her time. I hope I can be that way when I get older. I wonder how old she is. Let's see, service in Afghanistan. Is that what the guy said? No wonder she was so much in control. So, maybe four or six years there? He said "tours" plural ... so perhaps she is twenty-six or twenty-seven? I'll be twenty-two this June. Not that much older. Lona, what kind of name is that? She said she was Navajo. But "Johnson" doesn't sound like an Indian name. So, okay, perhaps part Navajo and part white? Why did Preston call her Pocahontas? She could have been Hispanic, or Italian, or almost anything with her light brown skin and full lips. No use asking him that question. I'll just keep my distance and try to enjoy the woods, and this will be over in two days. Camping tonight and tomorrow and then out of here.*

She walked on as the pack straps cut painfully into her shoulders and the sweat dripped out of her short hair into her eyes. She pulled out a baseball cap attached to the hip belt on the pack and used it to keep her hair out of her eyes. *Man, this pack is heavy. Good thing I've been running and using the gym at school. And all the kitchen and farm work at Berea seems to have helped me offset the hours of sitting on my butt. I'm so glad I went there. I'm going to miss my friends and teachers. Only six more weeks left after I return. Let's see: four more exams, one major paper, and I'll be the first one in my family to get a college degree. Mom and Dad will be so proud. Though Dad's questions about me and my boyfriends and children will probably just increase.*

And what am I going to do after I graduate? I don't have a job. Where do I want to live? I probably should have gotten my degree in nursing. Then I would know exactly what I am going to do for work. Jeez, I hated anatomy. I would make a lousy nurse. Despite Preston, I do love the woods and the satisfaction of making food grow. Really lousy planning, there, Allie. It's not like I have a family organic farm I can return to after college. Worst case, I can get a job on the farms at Berea. Well, since the boys have left me in the dust, I will probably have some free time to think about a plan for my future on this hike. I wonder how heavy their packs are. Preston loaned me this pack and he put in a lot of stuff he said was my share of the group stuff.

The wind was now stronger and colder. It was clear that a front was moving in, and Allie's stomach growled. While still out of sight of the others, she heard them calling out, "We're here." She squared her shoulders, determined to hide her fatigue, and walked into the campsite. There was a ring of stones for a campfire and the ground had been flattened for two or three tents so no one would be sleeping on a slope. The sun was setting quickly, and she gratefully dropped her backpack in the middle of the tenting spot furthest away from the fire circle. Preston called out, "Hey Allie, what took you so long? We can't get started without the pan and food in your pack."

Only two days, she reminded herself as she opened her pack and dug out the cast iron skillet and the food bags that held ice water and sealed hamburger meat. *That damn Preston gave me the heaviest items. No wonder my shoulders hurt.*

"Hey girl, get hopping. We'll need some dry wood and that skillet and hamburger over by the fire. I carried all the chips in my bag," Preston smirked as he pulled out the light potato chips and stuffed a handful in his mouth.

Only two days. I will not give him the satisfaction of seeing my anger. She remembered her Aunt Marge telling her, "Never give them the satisfaction that they are getting to you." *Thank goodness Matt doesn't treat me like they do.* At some level she knew Matt also would not be able to stand up for her and she didn't expect him to.

Allie thought of the men in her family. She believed Aunt Marge had married a bully. *And my dad? Was he a bully too? He wasn't until he got hurt and went on disability. Then mom had to take over and be careful to hide all that she was doing.* She remembered one of the few times she had disappointed her mother. She had talked back to her dad and her mother pulled her from the room and told her to never do that again. She remembered her mother saying in a tight voice, "You are not allowed to add to his shame."

Allie did not understand that comment until she later learned about the coal mines closing and all the economic powerlessness of the men who had once been able to provide for their families. Damn corporations, she thought. Now she used her anger to give herself the energy to drag in the bigger pieces of wood for the fire. She hurried to collect dry twigs and branches and dumped her final load of wood next to Preston. She knew he would want to be the person who laid the fire and started it.

"Would you like me to make the dinner?" she asked, keeping her voice neutral.

"Now you're actin' like the girl I remember from high school," he said approvingly. "I'll just get us started on our whiskey reward for a day of hiking."

"Perhaps Matt and I can put up the tents while the fire is making some coals for our cooking," she offered.

"Good idea. Yeah, we don't want to get caught out in the rain that's comin'."

Allie put up the tent she would share with Matt and gathered more firewood. She wandered into the woods near a lake that was wide enough to have some small islands off the shore. There was a clear trail leading from the campsite to the lake. She surmised that all the campers came here to the lake to obtain water. She made a note to make sure that all the water she collected got thoroughly boiled. Allie finally returned to the campfire and cooked the meat in the skillet she had carried. She ate her juicy hamburger as efficiently as she could. She was anxious to clean up the dishes and get into her tent to read. She wanted to be away from the pack of boys. She wanted to rest her aching back and join the world of her current favorite book. *Never leave home without a book*, she thought to herself. The boys were continuing to tell stories about their high school days, and Preston and RJ were bringing Matt up to date on all the gossip of the people they knew. Allie found herself only vaguely interested in who was having sex with whoever and wherever, and who got drunk and was drinking whatever.

She unzipped the screen on the small two person tent she was sharing with Matt. She took off all the clothes she had worn on the hike and stowed them in her pack, keeping on her underpants and pulling on her long- sleeved sleeping shirt that hung down to the middle of her thighs. She tucked her backpack under the tent awning to keep it dry if it rained.

I'm so glad I didn't forget to bring this little flashlight that is on the elastic head band. I wish I had owned one of these when I was hiding under my covers at night reading way past my bedtime. Oh, how many times did I lie to my mother about that? No lying required now. She scooched down in her sleeping bag and read until her eyes got tired. She laid the book carefully aside, closed her eyes, pictured that ranger one more time, and quickly fell into a deep sleep.

* * *

Allie woke up with a start. It felt cold in the tent, and she heard loud voices.

"Shut up. Just shut the fuck up, you faggot."

"Why do you have to be so mean? You know what you really want."

Allie sat up and then heard a sound like someone hitting a club against a tree. And she heard a noise like someone exhaling air and being in pain. Then it was silent. She unzipped her sleeping bag and moved to the entrance of the tent, listening intently. She called out, "Matt? Preston?" There was silence. She pushed the tent flap open and crawled out, searching in the darkness, but saw nothing. Then she started to walk slowly in the direction that she thought the voices had come from, and she continued to call out to Matt and Preston.

CHAPTER 3

Allie was running through the woods, dodging the trees and limbs as best she could. She was changing her direction frequently, slipping and falling. She no longer felt the sting of where Preston had slapped her. She heard him crashing through the woods, chasing her, and calling for her to stop. She kept running as silently as possible and then looked for a place to hide. She made herself small, pressing behind a large fallen tree, listening for the sound of him. Then she moved more slowly in a different direction carefully placing her feet, stopping, and listening until she could no longer hear him at all. The hail had finally ceased, and she could hear noises better now. But no sound of him, just her own ragged breathing. And she thought the night didn't seem quite as dark. Perhaps the moon might be making its way through the clouds.

All her awareness was now on the cold she felt throughout her body. Her night shirt was soaked, her arms and legs and bare feet were wet, and she had goosebumps on every part of her body. Her feet felt scratched and sore, and she was shivering. *Now what? I have no idea where I am. I can't go back to the camp even if I wanted to. I must get warm, and I must find help. I remember reading that if you're lost, you need to stay where you are, and someone will find you. Right, find me in a few days. I won't make it that long with this cold. I don't have any tools to make a shelter, no cave. I need to keep moving. I don't dare lie down and go to sleep. Perhaps if I can find the trail maybe I can find some of the other campers. I know there were other campers who checked in before we did. If I can get to one of them, they could help* me. Now she could see a few stars and she tried to pick one and go in that direction hoping to stumble onto the trail.

Sometime later she fell yet again. Everything she touched in the forest was cold and wet and slippery. Now shivering uncontrollably, she felt like giving up. Taking a shaky breath, she thought about praying. She felt embarrassed to ask God to help her. She remembered people saying in church that even if you're not sure if God is there or listening perhaps, he is. *How much worse can it get? Okay, God, I do need your help. And grandmother, if you are up there watching, I need your help, too. Perhaps, you and God?*

With great effort she struggled once again to her feet. She searched the woods for a direction, and she saw the faintest flicker of a light. She squinted harder and moved toward it. Hallucination? The tunnel thing? No, it seemed real; she staggered towards it, putting one foot in front of the other. She vaguely wondered why she was so dizzy, struggling to remain upright. She tottered forward, concentrating only on the light. Now she was sure it was a light. It was a camp area, there was a tent. She fell once more and tried to yell but her voice was faint. Then someone was lifting her, helping her as they both staggered toward the tent.

CHAPTER 4

Lona estimated she had been asleep for a few hours when she woke up. She noticed that the hail had stopped, and the wind was not as strong. She was worrying about that young woman again. But she remembered that she had checked out the group and everything seemed okay. She had crept near their camp, staying in the shadows, and watched the boys drinking and passing around a joint. In the tent furthest from the campfire there was a light suggesting that someone was reading. She had decided that Allie was safe and walked on another mile or two to set up her own camp.

Now here I am awake again and worrying, she thought, as she looked for the poetry book she had brought along. Good old poetry will put me in a sleepy frame of mind she reflected as she started reading. *Jeez, I really like how Mary Oliver uses nature to explain the world.*

Suddenly she was wide awake. She heard something moving outside her tent. She reached for her handgun and was leaning forward to see out.

"He.. he... help me." The words were faint and then Lona heard a sound as if something had hit the ground. She unzipped the front of the tent and aimed her headlamp toward the sound. She saw Allie, clad only in a wet night shirt lying about thirty feet outside her tent. She rapidly scanned for signs of anyone else and then hurried over to the limp, but shivering body. She did a quick search of Allie's arms and legs, and nothing seemed broken.

"I'm going to help you into the tent. Let me know if you feel any sharp pain," she said. Then, supporting her under both arms, she half carried, and half dragged her to the tent. It was not easy lifting and dragging Allie through the narrow opening. She had to lower the top half of her inside and then turn her and roll her legs in after. Allie was slumped on top of Lona's sleeping bag.

"What has happened to you?" Lona asked.

Through chattering teeth, Allie replied, "Light off, light off."

Lona turned off her headlamp and tried asking again, but Allie's head was wobbling. She decided that the major risk right now was her low body temperature. She reached into her backpack and pulled out a towel. She got the soaked night shirt off her as quickly as she could and started to dry the wet skin and hair. Allie seemed unable to assist. Lona rolled her off the sleeping bag and unzipped it fully. Then she rolled her into the open bag and closed the zipper as quickly as possible.

She knew that she had very little time to help Allie's body temperature get higher. She reached for her thermos which had some warm tea left in it. She held Allie close with one arm and guided the thermos as best she could to her lips. Some of the warm liquid got down her throat. Lona waited a few minutes to see if the symptoms would lessen. She tried to remember how long she could wait before she had to use more extreme measures. She realized Allie would not be able to create enough of her own body heat to get warm inside the bag.

Lona swiftly stripped off her thermal top and bottom and crawled into the sleeping bag with her. She wrapped her clothing around Allie's head and said, "I'm going to have you lie on top of me. We need to get as much of my skin on you as possible."

"I, I can't," Allie stuttered.

"You must," Lona said in her most commanding voice. "Your life depends on this. Think of me as a giant hot water bottle."

Allie allowed herself to be positioned on top of Lona. They were face to face with Allie's head hanging down on Lona's shoulder. Allie was stretched out along Lona's longer body. Lona tried to hold Allie's legs together with hers pressing them together.

Lona felt like she was hugging an ice cube, but she used her arms and legs to press the two women together and then she pictured having a fire inside herself. She said in the soothing voice, "I know this is hard. I don't know what has happened and you don't have to tell me right now. Just allow my body heat to come into you. You are safe. I will keep you safe and you will get warm."

Very slowly the shivers became less extreme and less frequent as Allie's body absorbed some of Lona's body heat. Lona knew the shivering would be followed by exhaustion. Allie's body had done everything it could to help her generate her own heat through her shivering.

"It's all right if you feel tired," Lona said. "You've been through a lot, but you're safe now, and you are getting warmer. It will be all right if you rest, and it will be all right if you fall asleep on this hot water bottle."

Lona could feel the ice cube getting less cold. She could feel Allie being able to relax and, sooner than she thought possible, Allie seemed to drop into an uneasy sleep, sometimes whimpering. With each whimper, Lona held her and patted her and made soothing noises and let her own rage increase her body temperature. Once she could feel that Allie's skin temperature was approaching hers, she took one arm out of the bag to make sure her gun was nearby. Despite wanting to stay awake and on guard, the relief of believing that Allie would not die of hypothermia quickly dropped Lona into a deep sleep herself.

* * *

Allie's Dream

I am running. I'm being chased by a monster, and I am so cold. I am wet, I am out of breath, I think I'll probably be killed. I see a small hole in the ground, and I go straight into it to hide. I press myself up next to the wall, becoming as small as possible. I'm trying to control my breathing so that I cannot be heard. I'm shivering, but I'm staying very quiet, and the monster runs past the entrance. I feel a little bit of relief but then I hear breathing in this small hole, and I don't know what it is. I am afraid again because I think it may be a bear. I think I am in the den of a bear. And then the bear pulls me onto her lap, and the fur is soft and warm, and I can feel the heat from the animal coming into me. The bear doesn't smell. It is just warm and breathing and comforting. And I feel safe. Then the bear moves my head to its nipples, and I think, does it have cubs here or in the den? But there don't seem to be any. I think she wants me to drink her milk, and I go ahead and try. I suck and I feel warm and safe and comforted.

And then the dream shifts, and the fur disappears, and now I'm being held by a woman. I'm too big for her lap and I'm lying on top of her, and her skin is warm and I am hugging her and, what? One of her nipples is in my mouth. And I seem strangely okay with all this because I am just so grateful to be safe and warm? And my body starts to get warmer, and I notice a lot of warmth between my legs. I seem to be getting kind of aroused and I am pressing my face between her bare breasts and I'm wanting to rub my body on her and she is moving under me and pressing her body on me. And this energy is in my hips and then I think I'm going to have an orgasm.

And then I jerk awake and I'm not in the dream anymore.

* * *

Lona's Dream

I am lying in bed and there's a woman lying on top of me. We are both naked and she fits very well on my body. Her skin is smooth and warm, and her face is near my breasts and then she puts her mouth on my nipple, and oh, I'm getting so turned on, so fast. I want to press all of my body on her and move her around on me. I am so wanting to press my hip up against hers and I start to do that, and now I'm trying to rub off on her. And I have my hands in her hair, and I am holding her mouth on my nipple.

Then I jerk awake, and I am not in the dream anymore.

* * *

Lona jerked to a stop. No more thrusting of her hips. She felt Allie making an abrupt movement to unlatch the breast as she said, "What? Wait! What's happening?"

Allie seemed as startled as Lona felt. With a hot rush of shame, Lona searched for words to try and explain their current reality.

"I, umm, I think we were both dreaming, and our bodies were just doing some, well, some things we would never do if we were awake."

"Oh, my God, was I kissing you? Like, like kissing your breasts?" Allie exclaimed. "That wasn't just a dream, it was real?! Oh, God, what is going on?"

Lona struggled to find the zipper to help both of them get some distance, as she searched for some more words. "Umm, it's, it's all right that you seemed to be doing that. I mean, it was a dream and no one's fault."

"Were your hands in my hair? Did I dream that or were you touching me?" Allie again asked.

"Well, I was dreaming my hands were in someone's hair. So, yes, I think it was your hair. I am so sorry. I feel terrible about this."

Both wanted out of the sleeping bag as fast as possible. And, of course, the zipper was stuck, and as awkward as the three stooges caught in a barrel.

"If you can shift off me, I can reach the zipper better and get us out of here," Lona finally said in as calm a voice as she could muster. *Dear God*, she thought. *I have turned this into a cluster fuck. I may have traumatized this young woman who has already been traumatized. I am not, not ever, supposed to take advantage of someone I'm helping.*

Allie tried to figure out what reality she was in. Oh, my God, she thought. I just had a dream of sucking a bear and then it becomes a woman, and then, shit, I was having sex with the ranger. What is wrong with me?!

Finally the zipper was found and unstuck and both women awkwardly disentangled their arms and legs and tried to get out of the bag without making any eye contact, and without looking at each other's naked bodies.

"Umm, if you stay in the bag, I'll get my clothes on and dig out some spare clothes for you, and then give you some privacy to get dressed. This tent is pretty small for two people." Lona pulled on her long underwear and a rain shell. She left her thermal top and some cargo hiking slacks in a pile for Allie, along with dry socks and some camp shoes. She quickly left the tent and noticed the sun was rising.

This is surreal, Allie thought. *And I have never had a dream like that. She must've started it and then I just of course went along and did what I did.* She felt immediately better once she decided that Lona had started it, and it wasn't her fault. But at the back of her mind, there was an uncomfortable thought that maybe she had started it. She'd been thinking all day of Lona. Not picturing sex, of course, but wishing she could get to know her. Wondering what kind of music she liked, wondering what books she liked, what movies. *STOP IT,* she shouted in her mind. *Get a grip. I am not a lesbian. I have, of course known some lesbians at college, and I am, of course, okay with them being that way.*

Allie went through all the accepting statements she could find about other people being allowed to be gay. Just not her. *And, just for the record,* she thought, *I am not interested in having sex with a bear. No bear sex, and no woman sex.* Somehow putting both bear and woman in the same "no sex zone" made her feel on safer ground.

CHAPTER 5

Both were quiet as they sat outside of the tent. Lona was staring out at the woods. Again, neither of them made any eye contact as Lona was boiling water over a small flame fueled by a canister.

"I packed some protein bars and tea bags, and you should try and eat something. And I'd like to know your name. I am Lona."

Allie shifter slightly to look at Lona. "Yeah, I remember your name from when we checked in. I am Allie, Allie Cooper. I would like some tea. I'm not sure I can eat anything just yet."

Lona filled a tin cup with hot water from a small pan that was sitting on the canister of compressed fuel. She handed it carefully to Allie and motioned to a pouch sitting on a rock. "Help yourself to a tea bag from that pouch." She had noticed some bruising around Allie's left cheek and eye. "I didn't notice the bruises on your face last night. Do they hurt this morning?"

Allie touched her face carefully, "No, they aren't too sore."

"I have some herbal medication for bruises that will help. It's in my first aid kit in the tent." Lona hurried to retrieve the pills as Allie stirred the teabag into a cup of the warm water. Their hands brushed as Lona gave her the pills. Both women felt an uncomfortable jolt and looked away from each other.

Lona cleared her throat again, and said, "I'm very sorry about last night. I never expected that to happen."

"Well, why did you get into the sleeping bag with me?" Allie asked.

"You stumbled into my camp and were sort of out of it, and I was very afraid that you might die from hypothermia. You were shivering, you were disoriented, your balance was off, your skin was very cold, and you had all the signs of extreme hypothermia. You couldn't produce enough body heat to get yourself warm and I believed that if I couldn't get you warmer you would die."

Allie took some time to take all that in. "Oh, well, thank you for saving my life. Actually, I really mean that. All I remember is some talk about a water bottle. Where did you learn to treat hypothermia?"

"I had EMT classes as part of my military police training. And we were told stories of soldiers in Korea and World War II who had to sleep together in the foxholes in order to survive. The warmer person has to use his body heat to warm the cold person and it takes longer if both of them are clothed. So I got you out of your wet clothes and I got out of mine and I stuck both of us in the sleeping bag."

Allie paused, "And the water bottle?"

"I was improvising there. I used that to give you instructions on how to treat my body and it seemed a safe analogy…"

"Do you think the soldiers turned it into sex?"

Lona took a deep breath to steady herself. "Of course, there was tittering and joking when the stories were told, but no one ever said that it became sexual. And no one would ever do it if it wasn't an emergency. And I don't think either one of us, as you said, 'turned it into sex'. Um, not consciously. Our bodies, umm, responded to those sensations and I guess we both made up a sex dream."

"Can we stop talking about this?" Allie asked.

"Of course," Lona said with relief. "But I do need to ask you, if you're ready, to talk about what preceded you coming to my campsite. And why did you keep saying, 'Light off, turn off the light.' You seemed very frightened and insistent about that. I assume whatever happened is related to the bruises on your face."

CHAPTER 6

Lona put a tea bag into the pan she had removed from the flame so the water could cool. She carefully took a sip. "Do you mind if I make some notes as you talk to me? Sometimes the initial report, being so fresh, has useful details," Lona said as she unfolded a small notebook and took out a pen.

"Sure, that is fine." Allie had rolled up the sleeves of her borrowed wool shirt and rolled up the trousers of the borrowed cargo slacks. The dry socks and camp slippers were keeping her warm and the morning sun was making the temperature comfortable. "Are you warm enough?" she asked Lona.

"I am. Just start at the beginning. When did you get into your camp?"

"I think the boys got into camp around 5 o'clock. I know it was still light. I was lagging behind because Preston had put all the heaviest stuff in my pack. When I got to the camp site, I looked for firewood and got the fire started and Matt and I set up our tent. Preston started drinking even before dinner. We cooked the hamburgers and ate them and afterwards I cleaned up and washed up a bit and then went off to the tent."

"Did Matt go to the tent with you?"

Allie sipped on her tea. "No, he got more wood and the fire

burnt down and they kept the bottle of whiskey going around, and I think they were smoking some joints. I went to the tent early."

"Do you recall what time you went to the tent?"

"Not really. I'd guess about 8:00. I had no desire to keep hanging around the fire with them. I read in the tent and fell asleep pretty early, perhaps around 8:30 or 9:00."

"When did Matt come to bed?" Lona inquired as she turned the page on the notebook.

"I don't know. I never heard him come to bed. I don't think he did. The tent is quite small, and I think I would have heard him if he came to bed. All I know is that I woke up when I heard some yelling. Maybe that was around 11:00 or 12:00? It was dark and I didn't look at my watch."

"Do you know who was yelling or what was being said?" Allie was silent and Lona sipped her tea waiting for Allie to find her words.

"It was Preston. He was the one yelling. He was calling Matt a pussy or something like that. And Matt was yelling back at him. Something like 'why are you so mean? You know you want to be different'. It was something like that." Allie looked away trying to remember.

"Do you have any idea what Matt meant?"

"Not really. Preston has always been quick to tease people about being queer and faggots and stuff."

"Do you think Matt might be homosexual?" Lona asked softly.

Allie paused and considered the question. "I don't know.

I don't think I ever really thought about it. I just thought he was a good guy. A smart and sensitive guy. He was my friend and loyal to me. He isn't as athletic as some of the guys, and he hasn't found a steady girlfriend yet, but that doesn't mean he is gay."

"No, it doesn't. Have you and Matt ever been boyfriend and girlfriend?" Lona asked.

"Matt is actually my cousin. And despite what you've heard about people from the hollers, we don't all marry our cousins," Allie said with some defensiveness. "Matt's mom, Aunt Marge, and my mom are sisters," she continued in a softer voice, "We were, like, each other's safe place. We both took the advanced level classes at school, and we had a lot of common interests. And we both knew we wanted to go to college and get out of West Virginia. That sort of set us apart from what many of the other kids were planning. It is kind of viewed as being disloyal to family to leave the town or the state. We were supportive of each other, and quite competitive with each other. Especially competitive with academics. I'd get the better grades in math and science, and he'd do better in English and history. Aunt Marge and Mom helped get us to college by sneaking us to a town where we could take the exams to qualify for college."

"Sneaking you?"

"Yeah, our dads didn't have much money and our moms had to save up money for the gas and the examination fees. So they kind of had to hide it."

Lona laid her pen and notebook down, "I can relate to family pressure to stay close. That is how it is on the reservation, too. Is it all right if we return to last night?"

Allie nodded and took a deep breath. "I heard this angry argument and then I heard a bad sound, sort of a sickening sound."

Lona waited. "Like if someone was hitting another person? Like a punch or slap?"

"No, more like a hit with a club. Like someone using a club to hit a tree or a rock. Allie closed her eyes.

"That is an awful sound," Lona said softly. "Take some deeper breaths. Can you describe what happened next?"

"I was scared and worried. And I got out of my sleeping bag and called out to Matt. And to Preston. No answer. Perhaps I also called out to RJ. And he didn't answer. I unzipped the tent and poked my head out, but I couldn't see anything. So, then I got out of the tent and started to walk toward where I thought the sound had come from. I was walking toward the lake, I think. Then a body just slammed into me and knocked me down and knocked the breath out of me. I realized it was Preston who had just tackled me, and he was on top of me. And he was, he was like crazy. Like a crazy wild animal. I was stunned and afraid. I tried to get out from under him. I tried to push him off me, and he was too strong." Allie stopped talking and looked away.

Lona waited.

"Can we call my mother?" Allie asked.

"We don't have any cell service this far into the woods," Lona replied. "And I know this is hard to talk about and to remember. But I do need to know what happened next so I can help you and perhaps help Matt, too…" Lona let the silence sink in. "Perhaps if you take some deeper breaths and picture the events like watching a movie, not actually being in the movie. Maybe that would help."

Allie looked off into the distance again and then continued. "I was yelling, and he grabbed both my wrists in one hand and held them over my head and then he hit me. I was stunned and I stopped yelling and fighting. He pulled my underwear down and he was trying to get his pants down and I realized what he was going to do." She paused. "He had his knees between my legs, and he was trying to spread my legs apart. I was calling to Matt and screaming, and he hit me again. And told me to shut up. I got quiet and when he took his hand away from my wrists and tried to get his … his penis in me. I rolled to the side and got one leg up and managed to get my knee between us, and I kept rolling and got to my feet and started running. And then I ran and ran."

Lona sat quietly, waiting for Allie to collect herself, to come back into the present. Lona cleared her throat and offered more hot water for Allie's cup. Allie shook her head and took some more sips of her tea. Lona was conscious of her own breathing, as she fought to manage her rage at Preston. "I am so sorry, Allie, for what you have gone through. Do you remember Preston saying anything besides telling you to stop yelling?"

Allie stared off into the distance again and was silent.

"Allie, Allie, try and stay with me here. Do you remember anything else that Preston said?"

Allie looked down at her hands. "I think he was sort of

muttering something like, 'Real man, bitch, show you a real man…' something like that."

Lona continued to write everything that Allie said.

Allie continued in a soft voice. "I, I ran. It was dark. I could hear him coming after me like a monster in a movie. I ran, I tripped, I hid. Eventually, I didn't hear him anymore. By then the hail had stopped and I couldn't hear much of anything. I was lost, and so cold. I told myself to not lie down. I thought of my family. I thought I was going to die. I prayed. And then I saw a small light and I just went toward that." She paused. "You found me, and you know the rest."

Lona wanted to hold Allie and comfort her, but she sensed that the comfort would not be welcome.

"We have to go back and look for Matt," Allie said. "We have to go back, and you have to bring your gun in case we run into Preston. I am so afraid for what he may have done to Matt. Matt needs us. We have to go back." Allie stood up abruptly.

"Right," Lona said as she stood and started to gather their breakfast gear.

CHAPTER 7

Both women worked silently as they rolled up the tent, packed away the sleeping bag, and stowed all the clothes in the backpack. Lona placed Allie's soaked night shirt in a spare dry bag keeping it away from the other clothes. She tried to separate her thoughts into different compartments as well. She worked to stay in her investigator role and not allow herself to linger in the personal compartment. Whenever she edged into the personal, all she felt was rage at Preston, admiration for Allie's grit, and shame about the dream.

"Ready to go?" Lona asked as she pulled the backpack onto her shoulder.

"Yes. Will you let me help by carrying the water?" Allie asked.

"Sure. Thanks." Lona slipped the full bottle of water out of the side pocket and handed it to Allie. They started down the trail leading back to the campsite Allie had fled.

"Let me go first," Lona said. "And just stay close. I suggest we don't talk so we both can listen for any noise of others on the trail. If I hear anything I'll just raise my hand and we'll both stop. Okay?"

Allie nodded. "How will you know if I stop?"

"I will be able to hear you if you stop." She saw the puzzled look on Allie's face. "I guess it is just from practice. I'm able to hear the sound of walking behind me and I always notice when it has stopped."

Allie thought of making a wise crack about "little miss bat ears," but she didn't know this stranger well enough to tease her and she realized she wasn't in a teasing mood anyway. She was walking with a sense of dread.

Lona walked for about 200 yards, letting her ears tune in to the sounds of the woods, and the sound of Allie's footsteps. She raised her hand and stopped and walked back to Allie and whispered, "You did great on watching for my hand signal. Now what I'd like for you to focus on, in addition to my hand signal, is the sound of the wind, and the sound of any birds. See how many different bird songs you hear and see if you hear any sound of water from any creeks we may approach. There will be a pop quiz later, so remember what you hear."

Allie was puzzled by these directions, but she nodded and softly said back, "Okay."

* * *

Allie noticed that her emotional meter was mostly stuck in "numb." She only felt feelings in response to Lona. She was reactive to her praise. And she felt safe as long as Lona was near her.

As Lona continued walking, she found herself being impressed by Allie's helpfulness, and her willingness to accept instruction. She also hoped that by giving her some assignments of listening and counting, it would help her with her intrusive thoughts about last night's ordeal and her projections of what lay ahead. She also reviewed the steps she would need to take to secure the crime scene. She regretted not having any of the proper equipment. She'd have to do a minimum of examination and figure out how to close off the campsite until the authorities could come and investigate. She hoped she could get enough cellular service to contact Jim once they got closer to the campsite. She wondered if Preston and RJ would be there. She didn't expect them to be.

Lona held up her hand and walked quietly back to Allie. "How many birds?" She asked quietly.

"I think I counted six different bird sounds."

"Very good," Lona whispered. "I counted six different songs, but one bird was a mockingbird, and he mimics the songs of others, so he did three of the six. And water noise?"

"There was a creek off to our left and I think it was responsible for all the water noise as it came closer, and then farther away from us. I heard it four times for shorter and longer periods."

Lona's eyes widened. "Damn, girl. You are good."

"My mother liked to use the word, 'precocious' for me. Are we close?"

"Yes. Two things are important now. Keeping you safe and keeping the campsite as clear of our footprints and any contamination as possible. We will approach slowly and quietly.

We will stop at the edge of the campsite, and I will watch it for some time and collect information."

"How will we find Matt?" Allie asked.

"You will call his name several times and if he answers, we go in immediately. And find him."

"What if Preston hears me and comes at us?"

"Oh, that will save us much time and effort. I would take great pleasure in arresting him. But guilty people usually run, so I don't expect him to be near us. If we don't hear any sound when we call, I will go into the campsite alone and look for any trail Matt might have left. I will mark my path with twigs. You will remain at the edge and within sight of me. If you hear anything, you can call me."

"But what if Matt is injured and needs our help?"

"This is the hard part, and you need to trust my judgement. I will go as quickly as I can go and scout for any sign of Matt. But I must be careful to not contaminate any evidence. We want to be able to prosecute Preston for what he did to you and what he may have done to Matt. I am better than average at reading footprints and trail. Once the technicians are here, they have all kinds of equipment that they can use. Can I trust you to follow my instructions?" Lona asked looking directly into Allie's eyes.

Allie was working to hold back her tears. "You don't think we will be able to save Matt, do you?"

"Sometimes I just have a sense about these things. I hope I am wrong."

"Okay," Allie said, her shoulders slumping. "Let's go."

CHAPTER 8

As the campsite came into view, they could see that both tents were gone, and no one was around.

"Why is my tent gone?" Allie asked.

"I suspect Preston got rid of it so that he can claim that you and Matt left the camp last night. Remember, he doesn't know that you are still alive. Okay, Allie, call for Matt now."

Allie did as she was asked. Each call getting increasingly louder. Each call separated by silence as they listened for any reply, no matter how faint.

Tears slid down Allie's face and eventually her throat was so choked she could no longer call.

Lona allowed some time for Allie to manage this wave of her anguish. Then, leaning forward she asked, "Can you point out to me the general area where Preston assaulted you?"

Allie took her time and then pointing out in front of herself, "Do you see that pine tree directly ahead of us?"

"The one beyond both tent areas?"

"Yes. About fifteen or twenty feet from our tent on an angle towards the tree is where I think he attacked me."

"Okay. Stay here and call if you need anything, or if you hear anything." Lona stepped from the trail and placed a twig upright in the ground by her first footprint. She had gathered two handfuls of twigs away from the camp site and then used them to mark her path to the area indicated by Allie. She walked slowly and looked carefully for other footprints and especially for any signs of blood. She found an area on the line Allie had suggested for the assault. The grass there was disturbed in a manner that suggested heavy weight had been on the ground. There were scuff marks at various points within the area and clear prints leading in one direction into the woods followed by other footprints following the first set. The footprints had long distances between them, suggesting that both sets were made by someone running. She assumed the bare foot marks were Allie's and the shoes following were Preston's. She went to the edge of the deeper woods and then returned carefully to the scene of the assault; certain she could now recognize Preston's distinctive sole marks.

Lona took a path parallel to his footprints that led to the assault area, and they too were spaced far apart. They confirmed her report of the collision that knocked the wind out of her. She could picture the struggle on the ground. She then traced Preston's running prints further away from the assault and she could see some blood splatters, and an area where the blood was the most pooled. She could also see signs of someone crawling away from one of the heavier blood splatters and then a cessation of the bent grass suggesting the crawl had ended. Preston's distinctive sole was present where the crawl stopped. The blood was most heavy in this spot. Then some more scuff marks and one set of prints leading towards the lake. The prints again were Preston's, and they were more deeply sunk into the soft earth. There were also some other footprints of a smaller shoe. Those prints seemed to be in a random pattern. Lona made a mental note to ask Allie if she had looked for wood near the lake. Near the water was more blood. Did Preston leave the body here for a while, she wondered. She carefully retraced her path and came back to where she could see Allie anxiously pacing and watching for her to return from the thicker foliage that surrounded the lake. She did not approach too close to the water as she was fairly certain that Preston had carried Matt towards the lake and perhaps dumped him there. She did not wish to further contaminate the crime scene. She now knew she would be calling the police and asking for divers and crime scene technicians with their access to luminal that would find even more blood and body fluids.

"Did you find Matt?" Allie asked in a soft voice as Lona approached her.

"No."

"Do you think he managed to run away like I did?" Allie asked hopefully.

"I couldn't see any sign of running into the woods except you and Preston. I did see some blood further towards the lake."

"Then where is Matt? If he didn't run and there is blood, where could he be?" Allie reached out and squeezed Lona's arm as she asked.

Lona stood still. "Once the crime scene people arrive, they

will be able to use their equipment to follow the blood much better than I can with the naked eye."

"Could Matt have fled into the water and gotten away?" Now Allie's grip was more urgent.

"I don't know, but again, the professionals will be able to find him if he is in the lake." Lona wanted to give Allie time to make her own way to the ugly ending.

All the strength holding Allie upright drained, and her body sagged. Lona reached out to support her and then slowly lowered her to the ground to rest against a tree. She stepped away and was grateful to see that she had some cell service at this location.

CHAPTER 9

Lona took out her cell phone, checking that she had battery left and signal.

Jim answered, "Hey, Lona, I've been trying to reach you. I know it's your day off, but those two boys, Preston and RJ, left and they are worried about Matt and Allie."

"Jim, they should be. Both Matt and Allie were attacked by Preston." She moved further away from Allie and lowered her voice. "I fear that Matt is dead. Allie managed to flee and was near death when she stumbled into my camp last night."

"What?!"

"Exactly. Are the two boys with you now?"

"No. They left perhaps two hours ago."

"Ahh, Shit. Okay." Lona paused to gather herself. "What category are we in with jurisdiction?"

"We are concurrent with the County Sheriff's Department. I usually call the National Parks' Investigative Services Branch to get them in the loop, but their staffs are so overloaded that they ask me to contact the locals for them to do all the forensics. ISB won't get involved until a body is found. The locals and we coordinate missing persons or lost persons investigations."

Lona responded, “We have one witness, Allie, and that should be enough to question them. We will need crime scene technicians and divers to try and find Matt’s body. Allie did not implicate RJ in the attacks, but he may be involved in the cover-up. Preston probably believes that Allie died in the woods trying to escape him. I think the information that she is alive needs to be protected in the initial interviews. Preston may incriminate himself if he believes she has died in the woods. Allie and I will stay here at the crime scene to protect the evidence. I don’t want her to walk back to the park entrance alone. She will need to give her statement to the police when they arrive. “

“Oh, Lona, I am so sorry for what that young woman has been through. Is she injured?”

Lona paced as she spoke to Jim, using her official voice. “She was hit in the face by Preston, and there are notable bruises. There may be others, but the hospital can document those. She is ambulatory and the attempted rape was unsuccessful.”

“Well, thank God for that. I don’t think I can get anybody there quickly.” He looked at his watch. “It will be at least two hours for the police and at least another two to four to round up the others. I’ll keep you updated on their ETA. Do you need anything else? Food, water”?

“We are okay with that, but I had to share my clothing with Allie, and she could use some of her own shoes and other clothes. I think she might be a size eight or ten, and shoes a size nine. If you can round up some of that from our lost and found bin. Or perhaps your wife has nearby friends?"

"I'll put her on it. She will like that task. And perhaps some of her homemade cookies. That helps everything."

"That sounds great, Jim. Pack some cookies for me, too."

"Will do. And, Lona, I am so grateful you were able to save that young woman. I will never doubt your instincts again."

"Me, too. Talk to you later."

Lona returned to where Allie was slumped back against the tree. She was familiar with the dead eye stare, having seen it in her military days. She moved slowly towards Allie, not wanting to startle her. She watched carefully for any signs of a negative reaction to her presence. When there was no sign of that, she lowered herself carefully next to Allie and used the tree trunk as a support for her back. She settled in next to her with their sides touching. Lona remained still and focused on her own breathing, trying to soothe herself in the presence of Allie's pain.

Eventually, Allie shifted a little towards her and Lona moved her arm around Allie's shoulder and accepted Allie's head resting against her. Now Lona focused on matching her breathing with Allie's. After a while, she was aware that Allie's breathing had deepened. Lona listened for bird and insect noises. Eventually, she found herself humming some of the healing chants she remembered from her grandmother.

* * *

Lona opened her eyes. She didn't move but she knew she heard other people approaching. She sensed that Allie was asleep. She realized that she had stopped humming and she felt rested herself. She started to carefully move and to wake Allie who was able to awaken without a startle. Allie made some noise like clearing her throat and then moved away from Lona. As Allie moved away from Lona's body, she saw she had made a drool mark on Lona's black thermal shirt.

"I think I fell asleep. And jeez, it looks like I drooled on you. I'm sorry," Allie said with some embarrassment.

"Lona gave her an awkward pat. "You know, Allie, everybody drools when they sleep." "Well okay, but I've never slept with anyone as an adult." She paused. "You probably think I am pathetic."

"No, I think you may be inexperienced, but not pathetic. We need to get up. I heard some noise of people approaching on the trail. It may be the police." She felt Allie stiffen as her body put on its cloak of fear and sadness again.

"Okay, they will want to question me, won't they?"

"Yes. You will just tell them your experience. In as much detail as you can manage. It will be all right if your feelings come out as you tell them what happened."

"I will have to re-live it again, won't I?"

"I am afraid so. But each time you put words to your experience, it tends to lessen the intensity of the re-living. At least that is what the books say."

"Have you ever had to tell people about some trauma that you've been through?" Allie asked.

"Yes, I have," Lona said in a soft voice. "I can share that with you if you want later."

"Okay," Allie said, and she rose to meet the two policemen approaching on the trail.

CHAPTER 10

The two men were dressed in the County Sheriff's uniforms. Lona noted that they had both worked up a sweat and concluded that they had done their best to hurry. The man in the lead appeared to be in his early to mid-fifties, a little overweight, but still fit-looking. Lona thought he had a focused look on his face, as he evaluated her as much as she was evaluating him. The man behind him was considerably younger, all muscle, and hyper energy. She guessed he was in training and that this might be his first experience on a death scene outside of vehicle deaths.

Lona extended her hand to the older man. "I am Ranger Lona Johnson, and I am glad to see you and I appreciate how quickly you have gotten here. And this is Allie Cooper."

"I am Sergeant Charles Kelly, and this is Deputy Bill Williams. Can you bring me up to speed?"

"Certainly. Last night around midnight, Ms. Cooper barely managed to make it to where I was camped about two miles further along the trail. She was hypothermic and bruised, as you can see, and she reported that she had been attacked last night by a young man named Preston Stuart. She and her cousin, Matt, were on a camping trip with Preston and a friend, RJ, and they were at this campsite. Preston had tried to rape her, and he had hit her in the face twice. She managed to escape and ran through the forest to my campsite. Prior to Preston's attack on her, she had heard Preston and Matt arguing loudly and she heard a noise she believed was the sound of a fight. She believes that Preston may have injured Matt, and we came here about three hours ago to check on that.

"I served as a Military Police Officer for six years in the army and I did a preliminary examination of this campsite. I have not touched anything in this site, and I have marked my footprints with twigs to expedite the crime scene investigation. There are several trails of blood and we have called for Matt and no answer. There are footprints and drag marks that suggest he may have fled or been placed in the lake just behind this camp. Since we arrived, no one else has been here at this crime scene." Lona paused to allow the men to absorb the information and to begin their part of the investigation.

Allie stood silently behind Lona looking off into the forest.

"Did you make any notes during your inquiry of Ms. Cooper?" the sergeant asked.

"I did, and I also took photos this morning of her facial injuries." I will forward those to you. I also have her clothing in a bag that I can give you or the technicians. Ms. Cooper is ambulatory and after you have all the information you need from her, I was hoping one of you could accompany her back to the Ranger Office where she can contact her parents and go to the hospital for further forensic photos and possible evidence collection. I would hope she will not have to stay here until the crime scene technicians arrive and process this area. I am unfamiliar with how the various agencies here handle and cooperate in a possible murder in this county. Jim, the Ranger in charge of this park, informed me that we have concurrent jurisdiction."

The sergeant gave a wry smile. "It can get kind of complicated when crimes are committed in a National Forest. But you and I will do our parts and people in some pay grades above us will manage the turf part. I am grateful to have someone of your experience here. Has Ms. Cooper bathed since the attack?"

"No. And she is wearing clothes that I loaned her for the walk back here, and my camp shoes."

"Jim sent me with a bag of clothes for Ms. Cooper, and some shoes. We will put the borrowed clothes in one bag and her clothes from last night in another bag and give them to the technicians. Hopefully they will provide some useful physical evidence. Bill, can you get two evidence bags from our pack? Ranger Johnson, would you help Ms. Cooper change her clothes, perhaps over there," he said pointing to some trees away from the camp site. "I'll get the paperwork started and take Ms. Cooper's statements once she has changed."

Lona led Allie away from the policemen and held out the evidence bag for her clothes as she removed them. Allie turned away from her for some privacy and Lona saw more scratches and bruising on her back. She did not comment on the bruises. She didn't want Allie to know that she was examining her body for further signs of the struggle with Preston, although she knew the observations would be part of her written report.

"Whoever got me these clothes did a good job of guessing my size. The shoes also fit. Why do they need the clothes you lent me?"

"Sometimes your body can carry something of Preston's DNA and that helps to document the rape." Both were awkwardly silent.

"Do I need to tell them we were naked in the sleeping bag?"

"That will be part of my report and will be viewed as it was intended, an action I took to help you recover from the hypothermia. And it will explain any of my DNA that may show up in the clothes you have borrowed. There will be no mention by me of the dream stuff."

"Good," Allie said with relief. They walked back to the officers.

"Okay. Let me get the paperwork started. Ms. Cooper, would you like to sit down while I ask you some questions? There seems to be a convenient log over here." Sergeant Kelley pointed to a log off the trail. "Bill, can you get the crime scene tape out of our backpack? Ranger Johnson, do you mind helping Officer Williams give us a good perimeter around this scene?"

"Certainly," Lona said. So far, so good, she thought, impressed with the sergeant's professionalism and calm manner.

* * *

After an hour or so, the sergeant motioned Lona over to where he and Allie were sitting. "I think I have all the information I need from Ms. Cooper for now. I can have Officer Williams take her back and accompany her to the hospital."

Lona saw Allie look at her with some alarm. "You won't be coming with me?"

"No. I realize I can be more help if I stay here and assist with the collection of evidence. You will be very safe with the Officer. He will absolutely keep you safe, and the hospital people will be helpful, I'm sure."

"I don't need to get any treatment from the hospital. I am okay."

"I misspoke. The hospital will collect evidence that will help in the prosecution of this case. Justice won't happen without evidence to support your statements," Lona explained.

Allie got up with a sigh and started down the trail. Officer Williams hurried after her.

The sergeant turned to Lona, "What have you not told me about the evidence?" he asked.

"First of all, I appreciate your discretion. I am hoping some of the details of Matt's death can remain hypothetical or delayed until later."

"Like what?"

I think Matt was struck in the head with a blunt object, but not immediately killed. There was a pooling of blood and then crawl marks through the weeds near the lake. I think he heard Allie calling during the attempted rape and tried to get to her.

He either bled out or Preston came back and finished the job. The autopsy report will help with all of that. The heavier footprints indicate Preston picked Matt up and took him into the lake. Also, the tent Allie and Matt were in has disappeared from this site. So, someone moved it, or it is also in the lake. These are unanswered questions. Also, you are from around here. Do you know this Preston kid?"

The sergeant stroked his chin in a thoughtful manner. "His dad is probably the most wealthy man in town, and will get him a good lawyer, I'd think. I don't know of any juvenile or criminal record, but the city cops would know that better than me. We've had so damn much drug abuse in our counties and that may have contributed to this mess. Allie said they were drinking a lot and smoking pot, but there may be more than that. Did Allie seem intoxicated or impaired last night?"

"She was definitely impaired from hypothermia: confused, dizzy, extremely low body temperature. I did not smell any alcohol on her last night. I was doing basic EMT stuff with her just to get her body warm and we had no coherent conversation until after she warmed up and slept some. I wasn't sure she would live last night. It was touch and go."

"That is consistent with her report," Sergeant Kelley replied, looking at his notes. "She said she thought she was going to die in the woods from the cold. She clearly had a gap in her memory from when she arrived in your camp and when she woke up this morning. The hypothermia can account for that."

He continued, "How about this Matt? What is your take

on him?"

"He is as clean cut as Allie. Both of them are college students. They looked out of place with Preston and RJ from the beginning. I started the check-in process with them and when Preston got inappropriately flirty with me, Jim finished the check-in. I was worried enough about her that I left early for my scheduled days off. I had planned to check some of the border areas of the park and just have some time alone. I walked by their camp site after dark and the boys were drinking, and it looked like Allie was in her tent alone. That was around 8:00 pm. I went on down the trail and set up in the next camp site about two miles away."

Sergeant Kelly was writing as fast as he could getting Lona's details into his notebook. "Did you hear anything from their camp?"

"No. I heard lots of wind and some hail and rain sounds, but nothing until Allie approached my tent and called for help and then she collapsed. As for Matt, Allie said she overheard some angry talk between Matt and Preston. And Preston calling Matt a pussy or something of that nature, I'd need to look at my notes for the exact wording."

"Yeah. She told me something similar. Here we are speculating on motive, but do you think there may be some type of homosexual panic thing going on here?"

"I have wondered about that myself," Lona replied.

"Do you think this RJ was complicit?" Sergeant Kelley continued.

"I have no evidence of that. My hunch is that he was basically passed out in the tent he shared with Preston. He didn't come help Allie when she was calling. He might be complicit in some cover-up. I think the initial interviews with them will be critical. Will you be involved in that?"

"They will probably bring in detectives from somewhere for that. It really will be a scramble once the body is found and ISB takes a bigger interest because of the National Park location. Hopefully the forensics will provide substantial evidence. But you and I will probably be stuck out here while the initial interviews happen. I have good relationships with the detectives who will do the initial interviews. It seems critical that they obtain Preston's clothes before he has a chance to get rid of them."

Lona sighed deeply. "I know. That is my biggest concern about the time frame for questioning him. Will you be here for the crime scene evidence gathering?" Lona asked.

" 'Fraid so," the sergeant answered. "Though I don't expect the divers to be here any sooner than tomorrow and they will need daylight, I think, to search the lake. If Matt isn't there, then they will have some dogs out. It is going to be a long night."

"I have a tent and gear and food and can keep the crime scene secure. Perhaps you could go back and keep the interview process and clothing search on track. There really is no reason for both of us to stay out here tonight," Lona offered.

"I was so hoping you would say that, Ranger Johnson. Do you mind if we switch to Lona and Chuck?"

Lona smiled. "I would like that, Chuck. Do I get to keep all the food that was sent with Allie's clothes?"

"All but the cookies," Chuck replied. "I want to split them."

"That's a deal."

CHAPTER 11

Lona took out her phone and called Jim again. He picked up on the first ring.

"Lona, glad you called. The crime scene people can't get there till tomorrow. Their equipment needs are excessive, and they are out getting ATVs to transport all of that up there. Same with the divers. Can you stay and protect the crime scene?"

"Yes. I had planned on that and have enough gear to be comfortable. I sent the Sheriff's deputies back. One with Allie to take her to the hospital and Chuck, the guy in charge, will also be coming back. We assumed the technicians wouldn't get here today. Chuck is going to try and help with the initial questioning of Preston and RJ. Please remind everyone that it is critical that the news of Allie's safety be protected until the initial interviews are complete. Oh, another thing. What was Preston wearing when you saw them?"

"Hmm. A hoodie sweatshirt with some rock band picture on it. And sweatpants. Why?"

"He was wearing that military camo outfit when he committed the crimes, and it will be critical to obtain those clothes for blood splatters."

"I can notify the Sheriff's department of that information so they can see if they can obtain a warrant to search for that."

"I think Chuck will let them know, but no problem if they hear it more than once."

"So you and Chuck got on a first name basis?"

"Yeah. He seems very capable and trustworthy. Not too concerned with turf battles."

"Right. That has always been my experience with him too."

* * *

Put one foot in front of the other, Allie told herself. *This is surreal. How can one day divide my life into a giant calendar? All my life before this one day and then my life after this day. I was one person before on this trail in the woods, and now I am on the same trail, but not the same person. I was irritated and annoyed, but I knew who I was and was facing a future that wasn't totally clear, but it had an outline. Finish school, look for work. Today I am numb and empty and … and broken. And I can't focus at all on my future and I'm not sure of who I am anymore. Okay. Count the number of bird songs. Listen for the sound of water. I wish Lona was here. She was something, someone to hold onto. Matt is no longer on this earth. I need him on this earth. He knew who I was. He accepted me. He loved me. He was the brother of my heart. We were a team against, well, against what? Other students? Our West Virginia bondage? Allie, that is too strong. Is it?*

And why am I picturing Lona now? Why am I remembering her voice? Her words that I am not pathetic. Why am I remembering waking next to her at the tree? Ohh, Shit!! Why am I remembering the dream and those sexual feelings?!! Listen to bird songs, count them, one foot in front of the other.

"What school did you go to, Allie?" the deputy asked.

"Please don't talk to me now," Allie said, walking faster.

* * *

Lona found a flat place on the ground and started clearing it of rocks and small branches. She moved automatically to set up the tent and felt some calmness in the ritual of making her camp for the night. *I need to give my brain a rest, she thought. All my speculation about Preston's actions is just rehearsing scenarios that may not match the evidence.* She focused on the details of unpacking her backpack.

Well, here I am now remembering carrying Allie into the tent. And I liked how she leaned into me as we napped at the tree. I like how smart she is. I like her grit and courage to fight and run and not give up. I like how she felt lying on top of me. In the tent. Oh shit!! No, okay, change that picture. Okay, back to looking at her bare back and the bruises. No… No.

So, if I am Preston, what would I do after I got back from chasing Allie…

CHAPTER 12

Preston sat on his bed playing a video game on his TV screen. His father opened his bedroom door with such force that it banked off the door stop. Preston jerked away from the screen and faced his father.

"What in the hell have you gotten yourself into?" he snarled.

"I, I don't know what, what you're talking about," Preston stammered.

"I got a call from a friend, and you will be brought in for questioning. That girl, Allie Cooper, has accused you of trying to rape her while you were on that camping trip. I thought you were going to be gone all weekend. What the hell happened?"

At 6'3" his father towered over Preston. His face was flushed, and Preston dropped his game controls and got as far away from his dad as he could on the bed.

"What? What did she say?" Preston managed to get out before his father slapped him across his face. Preston cowered, putting his hands up around his head to block any further hits.

"You fucking pussy. Get your head up and answer me," his father spat out from his clenched jaw.

"I, we, RJ and me, came back early because Allie and Matt left the camp early. I don't know where they went. It rained and was cold and miserable, so we just came back."

"Well, that girl has bruises and says she ran from you, and this Matt is missing," his father continued when Preston stopped for a breath.

"Well, maybe he bruised her. Maybe Matt did that. Why is she blaming me?" Preston shrugged.

"Evidently some park employee was nearby, and she helped her."

Preston's eyes widened. "It must have been that half-breed Indian. Lona, her name is. She had it in for me when we checked in."

"Whatever," his dad replied. "I will call our attorney and you are not to say anything to the police without him. You got that? You are a lousy excuse for a man You do nothing around here but drink and play those video games. And now you do this."

"Dad, I didn't rape her," Preston stated.

"Well, I don't believe half of what you tell me. But at this point, we need to get this mess cleaned up, and you need to keep your mouth shut. You got that?"

"Yes," Preston mumbled.

"You make me sick," his father turned and slammed the door on his way out.

CHAPTER 13

Lona finally woke up in her own bed at her sleeping quarters (as she called the Park Service housing). The wooden cottage, built by The Civilian Conservation Work Corp during the depression era was essentially one open room with a single bed. The only personal item in the room was her wool Pendleton blanket serving as a bedspread: white background with wide bands of color. The blankets were originally traded to Indigenous People in exchange for furs. A kitchenette anchored one wall with a hot plate and an under the counter refrigerator. There was a bar for her clothes that could be hung up, and a tiny bathroom with a shower, sink and toilet. She had not put anything on the walls. Along the other wall was a small chest of drawers, a battered desk and folding chair that served as her office. The only improvement was a chin up bar she managed to secure in the doorway to the bathroom. There were two screened windows that could be opened to catch a breeze, and a small space heater in the corner. A nightstand near the bed held her favorite books.

She looked at her clock. It was 6 PM. *Geez,* she thought, *I've been asleep for ten hours and Jim and his wife, Mary, expect me for dinner tonight at 6:30.* She hurried to shower and get to the house that was included as a benefit for the head ranger position at the park.

Jim answered her knock.

"Come on in, Lona, Mary is just finishing the cooking." He gave her a warm hug.

"Thanks, Jim. I didn't know how much I needed that."

"Yeah, I've been on body-retrieval duty, and it isn't easy. Let's help Mary bring the food to the table."

"I got this," Mary said as she entered carrying a heavy platter of a whole roasted chicken with dark brown crispy skin, surrounded by roasted carrots, onions, and potatoes. She set the heavy platter down and then approached Lona with her arms out, pulling her into a long embrace. Lona let herself linger next to Mary's softness surprised by her own willingness to be comforted.

After they disengaged, Lona realized she had never spent any personal time with Mary. She took in a deep breath enjoying the aroma of a home cooked meal, and then decided to also breathe in Mary. She saw the lines on her face created by smiles and not frowns. Her body was a comfortable size for a woman she judged to be in her mid-fifties, with some gray streaking in her hair. Lona saw tasteful make up in muted colors on her face that complimented her brown eyes, full lips, and round cheeks. She found herself liking Jim even more because of his choosing to be with such a comfortable, and, Lona assumed, a competent woman.

"Did you get some sleep?" Mary asked.

"Yes, I think nine or ten hours. The technicians finished

their work after the divers found Matt's body in the lake. I got in around 8 AM this morning and basically collapsed after being with them for two days. Have you heard any update from Chuck on interviews or hospital report on Allie?"

"Not much," Jim replied and seated himself next to the platter of chicken. "The hospital confirmed all the bruising you saw, and her feet were pretty damaged from her barefoot flight through the woods. Chuck told me Preston claims he was in his tent all night with RJ, and both of them assumed Matt and Allie had left early in the morning. RJ basically claimed he was passed out but says Preston was in the tent when he woke up."

"Did they find Preston's clothes?" Lona asked as she took an empty chair.

"No. He claimed he left them in a donation box outside a Salvation Army facility and that some homeless person must have taken them from the box."

"Shit."

"Right."

"Hey, you two, give yourselves some down time from the case and eat this dinner," Mary said in a commanding voice.

"This smells wonderful," Lona said, as she put a big helping of everything on her plate. "I can't remember when I've had a home-cooked meal. Oh, and is this bread home-made?"

"Yes, Jim got me one of those bread machines and we use it all the time now. And save some room for my apple pie later."

"Lona, I want you to come here a lot. She doesn't do this kind of meal just for me," Jim said with a wink at Mary.

"Well, it certainly beats the freeze-dried stuff I've had for the last three days, except, of course, the cookies you sent, Mary. They were the only bright spot I had for a while."

They all ate in silence enjoying the food and making small talk for the rest of the meal.

After dinner and the dishes got put away, Jim asked, "How are you really doing, Lona?"

"Good question. I thought I was all done with death and loss when I left the service. I spent several months after rehab doing the typical long hikes in nature to let my nerves return to normal. I liked the woods so much, I entered the national park service. And here I am now, mostly managing people and not much woods' solitude. I may not be cut out for all the people stuff. How do you manage all the people stuff, Jim?"

He smiled. "I joined the NPS for the same reasons – to be in nature and protect the animals in the woods. I still cherish the days I get to clear trails or just babysit the woods during the off-season. But being older now, I guess I have more patience with people than I did when I was younger."

"I'll say," Mary chimed in. "You used to be so irritable when you had too many days straight of managing check-ins and reservations."

"She's right, of course. And this may sound kind of crazy, Lona. I don't remember if I read this somewhere or put it together, being with Mary. But I think of life, basically, as being on a voyage, like a voyage on water. And most parts of the trip are boring or hard or sometimes frightening, and then there are these islands scattered about. And I never know when I'm going to come across one of them."

"Islands?" Lona asked, confused.

"Yep, islands. Like Mary. Mary has become a major island for me. Initially she was, of course, incredibly irritating, and annoying and would interfere with whatever it was I wanted to do..."

Mary interrupted him. "Except, of course, for the island of sex."

Jim laughed. "Well, you know how it can be when you are young. But Mary helped me kind of grow up and we'd talk, and I'd feel better and now, well, just being with her is this island of safety. Frankly, I don't know how anyone can do this world without a good partner. Or good friends, whatever the connection is. We need safe people."

Lona let this sink in. "How long have you guys been married?"

"Twenty-five years," Mary piped up.

"Wow." Lona realized she had never spent much time with a happily married couple.

'So then," Jim continued, "I learned how to get little island snippets."

"Snippets?"

"Yeah, like little moments. Like hearing a bird song, or seeing a family around a campfire, or, frankly, sometimes just a good cup of coffee in the morning. I kind of stopped all my narrative of complaints and all the little moments started to appear." He paused. "And," he said with a groan, "Mary made me read books about how to be a better partner and a better person."

Mary laughed. "We both are still a work in progress." She leaned over and kissed him on the cheek.

"I think I may be having an island moment right now," Lona said. "You guys give me some hope."

"You better get out of here before Mary makes you start reading some of her self-help books."

Lona and Mary both laughed. "Actually, I do need to head home. I haven't typed up my notes on the investigation. And Mary, I might want to borrow some of those books. So I can be a better partner if and when I get the chance."

'I'll drop off a couple of books at your place tomorrow," Mary said.

"And some left-over pie? I learn better when I have sugar in my body."

"You got it."

CHAPTER 14

Lona hit the send button and pushed back from the computer and stretched. She rubbed her eyes. It was past midnight, and she was tired. The report documenting her actions and what she had seen and what Allie had told her was long and tedious. She was recalling it in as much detail as she had noted and that she remembered. *It has been over two years since I've had to write this kind of report. Jeez, I am rusty. Do I want to continue this type of work? Do I want to stay in the Park Service? So much people management. Not as much woods management. Do I want to become an agent in the ISB? Be one of thirty-three special agents to cover the entire United States? Fly all over the country and work a crime scene basically all by myself? I am good at following a trail. And I like the puzzle part of solving a crime. But I don't like the people I am following. I don't want to keep living in the middle of that kind of job with the unhappy endings. Perhaps go to Alaska, lots of woods there. Guide rich people to kill animals. Right. Unhappy endings there. I would need an entire shelf of Mary's self-help books then. All I know for sure is that I want to call Allie tomorrow and see how she is doing.* She closed her laptop and went to bed, exhausted.

* * *

The next morning Lona called Chuck to see how the interview with Preston went.

"Anything in his interview, especially before he found out that Allie didn't die in the forest that tripped him up?"

"I am sort of embarrassed by how the initial interviews went. They were kind of perfunctory, and he got his lawyer involved very early. So he didn't provide much incriminating information," Chuck regretfully replied. "It was clear that he had been informed that Allie was alive. The initial interview happened after Allie was released from the hospital. So someone leaked that information. It was clear to me that Preston knew she hadn't died. He feigned surprise and relief that she was alive."

"Do you have any idea who might have done that?" Lona asked. She heard Chuck give a deep sigh.

"The list is potentially long. Someone from the hospital. Someone from the officers being sent out to the crime scene. Someone from our department. Hell, even Allie's family calling in relief that she was okay. We needed to get to him before he left the Park or before we started the crime scene investigation. I'm afraid not much stays a secret in these small towns."

"Damn. Did Preston have any wounds on his hands?"

"He had some slight bruising on his right hand which he said was from tripping on a root on his way out of the woods. RJ confirmed that he did stumble on the way out."

"Please tell me you guys have found his clothes."

"I wish. He said he dropped them off along with his shoes in the donation box by the building that has services for the homeless. Needless to say, they aren't there now. And, of course, there is no camera there. We will keep looking for them."

Lona was silent as she breathed deeply to control her anger. "Well, now we wait for the autopsy results and the crime scene analysis. Thanks Chuck."

"I'm sorry my report isn't better," Chuck replied.

"Me, too. But I will hold out some hope for the rest of the forensics to be complete. Talk to you later."

"Yep."

* * *

Lona got Allie's voice mail. "Allie, this is Lona. I'm sorry I haven't been able to get back to you before now. I spent the last two days working the crime scene with the forensic team at the camp site and not much Wi-Fi or power. I want to know how you are doing, and, well, just see if there is anything I can do to help you at this point. Give me a call or text if that fits for you."

Allie listened to her voice mail. She felt her heart rate go up. She had wanted to call Lona but didn't have her phone number. Oh, and she didn't have a phone because it was lost somewhere at the camp. She was glad she had given Lona her parent's number.

Do I want to talk to you? Hell yes. I've been waiting for three days to hear from you. Or from someone. She picked up her parent's phone and had to use the redial button because her fingers were shaking.

Lona answered the phone, recognizing Allie's number, glad she had put it in her contacts.

"Allie, thank you for calling me. I wanted to know what has been happening to you these last three days."

"Same for me. Did you know they haven't arrested Preston?!! What is going on? I'm afraid to leave my house."

Lona took a deep breath and paced in her small room as she searched for her words. "Has anyone from the Sheriff's Department contacted you?"

"I haven't talked to them since they asked me questions at the hospital. I assumed they would arrest Preston after I told them he assaulted me." Allie gripped the phone so hard her hand began to cramp.

"I believe they questioned him, and then they have been waiting to get more evidence about the crimes. Has anyone contacted you about Matt?"

"Not me, but Aunt Marge heard from them that they found Matt's body in the lake. I had expected that, but I was holding out some hope."

Lona could hear Allie's voice choking. "I don't know if you want me to fill you in on the process that goes with an investigation. I cannot give you details of the evidence, but you need to hear that I spent two full days and nights with eight technicians and three divers going over every inch of the campsite. All of them working hard to collect the kind of evidence it takes to leave no shadow of doubt about Preston's guilt. It will be perhaps two to four weeks on the data analysis and a few days on the autopsy. So I want you to know they are working hard on this."

"And you were with them all this time?" Allie asked, pacing in her room.

"Yes. I got back to my room around 8:00 am yesterday and slept for nine hours. Then I went to dinner with Jim, the head Ranger, and his wife, Mary, and then I had to type up all the reports which took me till midnight last night. I am just giving you these details because I want you to know why I have taken so long to call you. You deserve to know how many people are working on this. Even though it seems to you there is no progress."

"That is a lot to digest," Allie replied in a softer voice. "Thank you. I had no idea how much time this takes. I, I thought… well, um, I thought…"

"Allie, I have not forgotten you. You and this case are at the top of my priorities."

Allie started to cry softly. Lona was silent.

"Lona, these tears are mostly relief. We have just been so much in the dark here. Not knowing what is going on."

"I understand. The waiting is hard, and the Sheriff's office typically is instructed to provide NO details, because that can hinder the prosecution. How are your injuries, and will you return to school?" Lona inquired.

"Well, my feet have been the greatest source of pain. But I can limp around now. I think the adrenaline kept me from feeling them. My face has turned a colorful rainbow of red, yellow, and a creepy green. But the swelling is less."

"That's good to hear, I guess. But embarrassing to go out in public."

"Right. I don't want to return to school looking like this. Mom said she'll help me with make-up. Since Preston isn't in jail, they want me out of town to be safe from him or any of his family. We have our hands full keeping the men and women in my family away from Preston. There is a lot of anger here and we take turns reminding everyone that we don't want to go to jail. Literally my mom and dad have both taken turns blocking the door from the other."

"You haven't tried to get to him, have you?"

"No, I vented in my room. It isn't pretty. Some furniture has been broken."

Lona found herself smiling. "Well, I can relate to that. I've always found it useful to let out some of my rage."

"Really?"

"You bet. So, school. How far away is it and have the police told you that you can't leave the county?"

"No, I think they want me and my face to leave, to not show up in town. In West Virginia, we have sort of a reputation for vigilante type of justice. School is about three hours away by car, but ten hours or so by bus. My dad can't drive that far because of his back and mom doesn't want to leave Aunt

Marge to handle all the funeral stuff by herself. I don't want to be on a bus with this face. I don't know if I can concentrate on schoolwork anyway."

"It might be good for you to be around some friends," Lona offered, carefully.

"I am tired of talking about this. I don't want to answer all the questions my friends would have."

"Hmm. Perhaps I could help. At least with the travel part. I still have some time off owed to me. I could drive you there. How soon is the funeral? Do you need to stay for that?"

"Mom and Aunt Marge say I don't. I'm not sure I want to go anyway. And really, the sight of me at the funeral might not be good for all of Marge's family. There is a lot of tension about all of this in our small town."

Allie continued "Let me talk to them about you driving me. I know they would trust you and they want to meet you and thank you for helping me."

"Okay, just let me know and I'll fill up the gas tank and we'll get you out of town."

* * *

Lona paced in her room and hit the return button on Chuck's phone call.

"Hi, Chuck. Thanks for returning my call."

"No problem. How are you doing?"

"I've been burying myself in physical labor. Lots of trail repair and camp site cleanup."

"Yeah, the waiting for forensic results is hard. Sort of like waiting to see what Santa will bring us. You know what I mean?"

"I do, "Lona replied. "Will we get the gift of hard evidence so we can nail the bad guys?"

"Exactly," Jim concurred. "So the autopsy is complete and the body has been released to the family." "Are you allowed to share the results with me?"

"Yes, since you are now the official lead person for the local park service. By the way, the deputy in charge of the crime scene wants to hire you on all the crimes committed in forests. He says he has never seen anyone track as well as you. Hell, he wants to have you on crime scenes anywhere."

"He'd be disappointed in my work in city environments. Can't track there unless there is snow or mud," Lona replied.

"Oh, and the detectives like your written report," Chuck continued. "Any chance you'd be looking for a different employer?"

"Not immediately. And I am not sure about my future right now. But daily investigation of crimes isn't what I want, at least not now. This death of Matt, and Allie's suffering are really affecting me. I seem to have recovered from the numbness of the war and I don't want to return to that."

"I can't say I blame you."

"So, Chuck, the autopsy?" Lona inquired. "Okay. The victim died of one blow, blunt force trauma, to the lower right occipital lobe. No wood fibers in the wound. So perhaps the weapon was a rock or something metal. Too much force to be a fist. The angle of the blow suggests a right-handed assailant. The death was not immediate, but it did occur before the victim was put into the water. No sign of defensive wounds to the hands or any other significant bruising or blows to other parts of the body. There was dirt under the victim's nails and his own blood mixed with the dirt, which would be consistent with him dragging himself before he died. There were traces of semen on his clothes. Some of it is the victim's and some is unknown. The detectives are obtaining warrants to test RJ's and Preston's semen."

"Thank goodness for that," Lona responded.

"Preston is pretty slick, and his lawyer is capably protecting him, but I think the judge will grant the warrants," Chuck continued.

"Great. If Preston had semen on Matt, it might help with motive. And it certainly gives him something he has to explain," Lona replied. "Any progress on finding Preston's clothes?"

"We're at a dead end with finding the clothes. Preston's claim of leaving it in an open box at a nearby building that serves a lot of homeless people is suspicious as hell, but hard to disprove."

"And Allie's clothing and blood?"

"That all went to the forensic lab along with the other one hundred or so bits of evidence. That will be weeks to process."

Lona groaned, "I'm afraid Matt's blood would have gotten

transferred to her night shirt during the attempted rape."

"Yes. I'm sure his attorney is hoping for that. It is a dream piece for raising doubt about who killed Matt. And who tried to rape Allie."

"Did the autopsy venture an opinion about time of death?"

"Yes. But it is so broad because of the time in the water that it can't rule out anyone. Basically, it was 10:00 pm to 4:00am. If it goes to trial, it will be a windfall for all the crime scene experts."

"Shit," Lona mumbled.

"Right. How is Allie doing?" Chuck asked.

"I called her a couple of days ago and she will be returning to school tomorrow. It seems your guys and the town police aren't crazy about her coming to the funeral all bruised and battered."

"Yeah. That could turn into a bad confrontation between the two families, with lots of young male cousins and uncles, drunk, you name it. Bad scene."

"Dare I mention Hatfields and McCoys?" Lona asked.

"Not if you want me to be your friend. We are so tired of that. The problem is that with all the poverty, depression, and addiction issues, we still sometimes behave that way. We just don't like outsiders teasing us about it."

"Chuck, I should be the last person to tease about that. I'm from the Rez, right? We have our own version of vigilantism. It is called 'Tribes.'"

"I thought all you guys were brought together on the same team by your mutual enemy, the US government."

"On the surface, yes. But certain tribes have been at war with each other before the cavalry came onto our land. Some tribes were working with the Spanish for a couple hundred years stealing women and children and selling them as slaves. And certain tribes worked as scouts for the cavalry."

"Clearly, I haven't read enough history of your people," Chuck interjected.

"Same here. I didn't know anything about West Virginia until I arrived here two months ago. Jim had to correct me that West Virginia isn't even considered part of the south because it wasn't part of the confederacy."

"Right. Everyone from the north gets that wrong."

"Why weren't you part of the confederacy?" Lona asked.

"We never had enough farmland to make having slaves profitable," Chuck replied. "And Virginia wouldn't even let us vote even though we were part of Virginia, because our farms were too small to qualify for voting. Then Virginia came and tried to use force to get all our sons to join their army. So, we seceded from Virginia in 1861 and Congress accepted us as a state in 1863 after the Civil War had started. Here in West Virginia, we sort of hate everyone else, but our own family clans."

"Jeez. Now you are really sounding like the Rez. Which, by the way, is just the Navajo reservation. I have four names: Lona, is the name that I have for school and for white people to address me. Then I have three Indian names: The first is the name of my mother's clan, followed by my father's clan, and then both grandparents."

"That has got to be a mouthful," Chuck ventured.

"It is. But it is useful on the reservation. My grandmother holds the record for being the oldest process server ever, like at age eighty. When I'd go out with her to serve a subpoena, she'd call out her clan names and we never got bit by the house dogs or shot by the person being served. Often, we'd get invited into the hogan or house and get freshly baked treats."

"That wasn't dangerous for you as a kid or your grandmother?"

"My grandmother's clans were big and if something happened to her all her clan would demand retribution. Oh, and my grandmother was scary fierce until the day she died. And she also had the reputation of being in pretty good contact with the spirits of the ancestors."

Chuck laughed. "What a sight the two of you must have made."

Lona sighed. "Looking back, I think we were a force to be reckoned with."

"Note to self: Don't ever cross Lona."

Lona chuckled. "I'm working on my fierceness. Umm. I hope this isn't a problem, but Allie has no easy way to get back to her college in Berea. It is only a three-hour drive, but her dad can't drive because of back issues and her mom has to help her sister with Matt's funeral. The bus service would take about ten hours and she doesn't want to be in public that much with her face all bruised. So I volunteered. I know the rules about no discussion of any of the evidence."

"No, that is okay, but thanks for keeping me in the loop. That family is going through a lot. And, Lona, thanks for all your help."

"Same back at you. Take care."

"You too."

CHAPTER 15

Lona parked her Jeep on the road outside Allie's house at 8:00am. She wanted to get an early start. Allie and her mom must have been waiting by the window. They hurried out to greet her. Lona noticed that Allie had a lot of her mother's coloring – blonde hair and blue eyes. Mrs. Cooper had gray mixed in with the blonde, and she was heavier, but still an attractive woman. She swooped in and embraced Lona in a full-frontal hug. Lona just surrendered to the force that would not be denied. As Mrs. Cooper finally pulled back, she held Lona at arm's length and looked her square in the face. "Thank you for saving our daughter."

"Well, your daughter did all of the hard work in just getting to me. But I was glad I was there. I am so sorry for the loss of your nephew. Did Allie share with you how many people are working on this and why it is taking so long?"

Mrs. Cooper let go of Lona's hands and took another step back. "She did. And it is hard to stay patient with that, but we know we must. I will rest easier when Allie is back at school."

Lona nodded and followed Mrs. Cooper inside. Allie hung back. Lona thought she seemed shy or anxious. She shot her a glance that she hoped was reassuring.

"Richard, Ranger Johnson is here," Mrs. Cooper announced as they entered the living room.

Lona approached a man who looked considerably older than his wife. His shoulders were broad, and she imagined that he had once been athletic. His injury and weight gain had taken its toll. She could see how painful it was for him to get out of his recliner. He stood and waited for her to approach, and she did, holding out her hand.

"Mr. Cooper, I am Lona and I'm glad to meet you."

He took her hand in his and held it, looking her straight in her eye.

"I cannot express how grateful I am that you saved my daughter."

Lona could see tears at the corners of his eyes. "I cannot begin to imagine what you have been going through with all of this. I am grateful that I was in the right place at the right time. And as I told your wife, Allie did all of the hard work in getting to me."

'I want to kill him of course," Mr. Cooper said with a tight voice.

"Me, too. I've thought of three ways," Lona replied. "How about you?"

His face remained tight. "Four."

"It takes a lot of energy to manage that anger. I've been out chopping trees and clearing trails and sweating," Lona offered.

"What I wouldn't give to be able to work it off that way," he acknowledged.

"Yes, you are in a very hard chapter right now. Shall we sit?"

He seemed grateful to lower his body back into his recliner.

"This may sound trite, but Allie is lucky to have parents who feel as deeply protective as you and your wife. I know this is abrupt, but we are hoping to get on the road early today, if you don't mind us getting out to the car."

"Of course. I know Lois has made up some sandwiches and cookies for you to take with you, so don't forget those," he replied.

"Great. I hope to have more time to get to know both of you in the future. Allie, are you ready?"

Allie hugged her mom and kissed her dad on the cheek and hurried out the door. Lona took the food bag from Lois and followed her out.

As Lona drove off, she glanced at Allie, "You seem kind of relieved to get away from home. Am I missing something?"

"Sometimes with my dad, well, it can be kind of socially embarrassing. He is in so much physical pain and so isolated, that I try and not introduce new friends to him anymore."

"He seemed appropriate with me," Lona said as she turned onto the highway.

'Yes, he was. I think he respects you."

"Even out of my uniform?"

"Lona, you sort of always seem to be in uniform, even when you're not."

"Really? I'm not sure how to take that." Lona glanced over at Allie.

"It isn't a criticism. It is just that you kind of emanate an aura of control."

"Hmm. Is that off-putting for you?"

"Well, not when I am needing rescue, it isn't. But perhaps on this trip we could have some sort of getting to know each other that isn't life and death stuff."

"Oh, like what friends do at the beginning?" Lona said with a small smile.

"Exactly."

Lona took a deep breath. "I sort of suck at this, but here goes. What kind of music do you want me to turn on? Or do you want to tell me some of your favorite memories of Matt? Sort of your own memorial service?"

"Let's do Matt's favorite music, which is country, which I used to tease him about. So let's turn on one of the fifty country stations and make fun of the music together."

"Okay, but just so you know, Allie, I do like Garth Brooks and Emmy Lou Harris and, actually, Dolly."

"Get out.!!! I like those same three," Allie exclaimed.

"Well, there you go. I'll keep driving and you work with the radio."

Allie noticed that she kept sneaking looks at Lona who was dressed in faded jeans and a white shirt with the collar unbuttoned. She thought the white looked nice against her light brown skin and dark hair. Today it fell softly to her shoulders, and she occasionally pushed some of it behind her ears. She liked the small silver and turquoise earrings. She thought Lona looked softer, and perhaps more relaxed.

"This may seem a little insensitive, but how did you get some curl in your hair? Allie asked. "I thought Indigenous

People all had straight hair, and brown or black eyes." Allie inquired, lowering the radio a bit.

"They do in the movies. But we are kind of a mongrel group. There is a lot of Hispanic DNA in us from the couple hundred years of the Spanish occupying our lands in the southwest. My family has lots of Hispanic first and last names. I always assumed the curl was from the Hispanic in me. And my eyes seem kind of mongrel, too. Sometimes they look green and sometimes kind of gold. I think the eyes are from my dad."

"Yeah, Johnson doesn't seem a Hispanic name," Allie ventured.

Lona smiled. "No, that is my very white father's name."

"Was he abducted by your people and raised as an Indian?"

Now Lona came out with a big laugh. "Yep, we got him off a wagon train in Utah from the Mormons, after we killed and scalped his parents." After a moment, she continued. "My dad was working with the Department of the Interior, acting as a liaison with the Health Services Department. Health Services has always been abysmally underfunded on the Navajo Reservation. He was there working with my mother, who was a nurse, as well as on the Indian Affairs Council. They fell into lust, and I am the product of that."

"Into lust is a rather strange way to describe your parents' meeting."

"It is how I think of it. The affair was sort of brief, though very consensual. No one in my family spoke poorly about him, but no one really knew him that well, and he was kind of a member of the government, which has a bad reputation with our people."

"Did they get married? Is that too personal?" Allie asked.

"Sort of, but hey, we haven't had the most casual of relationship ourselves." Both became very silent.

"I didn't mean that to sound that way," Lona continued. "I meant; we've been dealing with a lot of emotional stuff. Like two people thrown into the foxhole together. Shit. I didn't mean that either. Let me catch my wits here." She took a deep breath. "Okay, sometimes people are dealing with such extreme circumstances that their friendship gets jump-started."

"I like the way that sounds. Yes, jump started. Surrounded by such intense feelings that it doesn't progress in the normal way," Allie added.

"RIGHT."

"So, can I ask about your dad?" Allie inquired.

"Sure. He got transferred back to D.C. Mom didn't feel like she could leave her people and her life to be with him and he didn't want to leave his life and career and the city. He sent birthday cards and always a Christmas present, typically a present that had nothing to do with my life. Which, of course, he knew nothing about. Not his fault really. You don't get much different than DC and the Rez. I think he sent some small amount of money. My mom was very proud and self-sufficient, and she actually banked the money for my future."

"Is she still working?"

"No, she was killed in an automobile accident when I was eleven."

"Oh," Allie said in a soft voice. "I am sorry. That had to be very hard."

"Here's the turn-off I've been looking for," Lona said, turning on the signal and steering the car onto a road leading into some woods.

"Where are we going?" Allie asked looking around at the scenery.

"I thought we could stop by a water fall I've heard of and eat our lunch."

"Sure," Allie said, thinking to herself, I guess that is it for my personal questions today.

* * *

As they were putting the lunch and water into the daypack Lona had brought, she said, "Of the songs we were listening to on the radio, I think I liked that Gatlin Brothers song about gold in California the best. And the Dixie Chicks' 'Wide Open Spaces.'"

"I like both of them, too," Allie replied.

"Allie, what do you like best about them?"

"The harmony. The vocals are primary over the instruments."

"I had never heard of the Gatlin Brothers," Lona responded.

"Most people haven't, but my parents liked them a lot. I think it was also because their vocals and harmonizing were so prominent. My mom met my dad in church choir in high school, and she was a choir director for our church for as long as I can remember. So when the Gatlin Brothers sang, my parents sang along with them. They both had such good voices. The down side of having the church choir director for a mother was there weren't very many late Saturday nights out on the town. I always had to be at the morning service for church on Sundays."

"That sounds like a significant restriction to a social life," Lona said as she continued to pack.

"Well, our town was so small that the social life was restricted to pot and alcohol parties in the woods or people's houses with lenient parents. By the way, Lona, you have a nice voice and good pitch too," Allie said as she adjusted her shoestrings.

"Thank you."

"Did you sing in church or school?" Allie continued.

"No. Just lots of singing with the radio."

"That's pretty impressive that you could hear all the harmony and sing parts and not just the melody."

"I know. I always assumed everybody could do that if I could. But I've been around enough people now to realize not everyone can sing and sound good."

"Did your parents sing?"

"Both did. My father was in some fancy choir at Yale, they were called the Whiffenpoofs. He had lots of music lessons as a kid and his voice is amazing. Kind of embarrassing to be with if he starts singing in public," Lona paused. "And what's with you and those shoestrings?"

"Oh, my toes get easily cramped so I make the toe box as wide as I can and tie that off so I can tighten them around my ankle. Back to your dad. So do you guys ever sing together?"

"Nope" Lona was now looking for the trail sign to the falls. "Oh, there it is," she said as she pulled the daypack onto her shoulders. "The organized singing on the Rez were chants that have been passed down to us from a long time ago. Chants for healing or celebration or for the passage after death."

"Like to go to heaven after death?" Allie responded.

Not really, Navajo beliefs are kind of complicated. We have three souls, one of which can communicate to us and others through dreams. Mostly I try and absorb the beliefs through the lives that my mother and grandmother lived. They were always available to help others. And they were thoughtful people. They needed to be thoughtful because both were what you'd call strong-willed. Growing up I mostly was trying to not get on the bad side of my grandmother."

"Was your grandmother hard on you?"

"I said bad side, but I mostly mean I respected her so much. I did not want to disappoint her. People said of my grandmother that she 'walked in a good way'. Sort of like she was very aware of how to be a good person. And it showed in her actions. Like I said, it is complicated. Are you ready to go?" Lona asked walking toward the start of the trail.

"Yes. I realize I came here once on a school trip. After we get through these Wolf Trees, we will be in an old growth forest."

"Wolf Trees?" Lona raised her eyebrows.

"That's what they are called in Kentucky, at my college. They are the trees that need more sunlight as seedlings, and they can get more sunlight when there is a road that borders an old growth forest. As we get farther from the road, they will thin out until we will be in the part of the forest that is in climax."

"Wait," Lona said, "I thought I was supposed to be the expert here, RANGER Lona Johnson, and here you are teaching me stuff about Wolf Trees."

"Oh, I'm sorry," Allie hurried to say.

"Allie, please, don't ever apologize for being the smartest person in the room, or I guess, forest."

"Umm. Okay."

As they walked deeper into the woods, they soon became surrounded by a stillness. The forest was layered. On the ground were pits and mounds covered by thick moss. Large fallen trees also lay about the floor. Many of them serving as the beds of new saplings. The highest branches filtered the sunlight through bright green spring leaves. Large tree limbs entwined with each other stretching high over their heads. The middle space was taken up by various younger trees sheltered by the canopy and reaching up towards the sunlight. These saplings would eventually replace the older trees when they fell.

"We are catching the forest just as it is bursting with the bright green of spring," Allie said. "And the sky is such a bright and clear blue, what we can see of it."

They walked further on, and Lona paused and pointed to a light green moth hovering on a nearby fern covered mound.

"That is a Luna moth," Allie whispered, coming up quietly behind her. "They only live seven to ten days and mostly are nocturnal. They have no digestive system, so they live off the fat they accumulate as caterpillars. They mate and they die."

They stood silently and watched.

"Is this as special as I think it is?" Lona whispered back not wanting the moth to fly away.

"Well, I have only seen one other one in my life. So, yeah. This is as special as you think. And that flower it is near is called a Jack in the Pulpit, and they don't last very long either." They watched silently for some time and then the moth flew away.

"Hey, buddy, I hope you get lucky tonight," Lona said softly.

Allie felt her throat tighten. She took a deep breath. "John Muir said, 'Into the forest I go, to lose my mind and find my soul.' Thank you for bringing me here, Lona. I need to be in these woods today."

Lona gave Allie's hand a gentle squeeze. "Ready to go on?"

"Yes, absolutely."

They walked on in silence, soaking in the stillness, broken only by the chattering of the squirrels. Occasionally, a soft wind would reach their faces, carrying the musty smell of the decaying leaves and moist earth. Eventually they started to hear the sound of falling water and they came to a clearing at the base of a waterfall. Lona placed her pack next to an old firepit left by other hikers. She started to remove the food and other items.

"What is the book you're carrying?" Allie asked.

"Oh," Lona tried to hide it but then decided to show it to Allie. "Promise you won't laugh?"

"Sure."

"It is a self-help book."

"What?!"

"You said you wouldn't laugh."

"I'm sorry," Allie hurried to say. "I was just surprised. Not laughing. It's just that I think of you as so accomplished and all together. I'm just surprised. Sort of like seeing General Patton or Geronimo or someone like that pulling out a self-help book."

Lona took a deep breath. "I don't feel like I have it all together. I have been told I sort of have that style. I had dinner a couple of nights ago with Jim and his wife, Mary. And I felt such an envy for their relationship. Married twenty-five years and playful and loving. And I realized I haven't been around a couple like them very much. Maybe never. Some of it is my age, of course, but I've been with some older couples, and they didn't have the same energy as Jim and Mary. They told me that there were some books that helped them make their relationship better. So I thought, hey, read whatever they are reading to help myself become a candidate for a good relationship."

Allie was silent.

"Oops, too much information?"

"No," Allie replied. "I realize I haven't been around too many marriages I'd want to be one-half of. Can I write down the title?" Allie asked, pulling out a small notebook and pencil.

"Sure." Lona handed it over.

"What is that thing with the elastic band sticking out?"

"That is my sling shot."

"Sling-shot? Will we need that for our lunch? You know my mom packed enough for two meals for both of us."

"It just is always in any pack that I take into the woods, like, there is a small first aid kit, and an emergency blanket, and pills to purify water."

"And what does the sling shot do for you in an emergency?" Allie asked turning it over in her hands to inspect it.

"I can kill small game and birds with it."

"You're kidding. Right?"

"No. I could kill squirrels or rabbits, some ducks, perhaps grouse."

Allie laughed, clearly not believing her. Lona took the sling shot from her hands and walked around picking up small stones.

"Pick a target," Lona said.

"That tree stump over there," Allie pointed to a stump about ten yards away.

Lona pulled the bands back and released the pouch containing the stone. There was a loud thwack as the stone hit the center of the stump.

Allie ran to a tree limb further away and hung her baseball

cap on a branch. She was taking some steps away from the hat when it flew off the branch.

"What is the smallest thing you can hit?" Allie asked.

"Red leaf," Lona said as she pulled the band fully back and released the stone. The leaf fluttered to the ground.

"Okay and wow. How did you learn that?"

"I had a misspent youth," Lona said, smiling.

"Please tell me about that," Allie said as Lona sat down on a log and put the slingshot in her pack. Allie started to unwrap the sandwiches.

"Well, before I went to live with my father, I was mostly being raised by my grandmother. I spent all my free time running with a pack of boys on the reservation. We spent all our time climbing and hiking and getting into mischief. One summer all of us had all made ourselves slingshots and basically terrorized each other and anything that moved. I don't know how we managed to not blind each other by mistake." Lona reached for the sandwich Allie was holding out to her.

"Anyway, one day I had finally shot a squirrel and I ran home to my grandmother, so proud and wanting her to cook it. She was in the kitchen and when she saw me holding up the squirrel her face changed. A deep furrow came between her eyes, and it was like a black storm covered her face. Taking a very deep breath, she asked me if I had killed a squirrel with my slingshot. I was very scared of her face, but also very proud.

"'Yes, I saw it sitting on a log about twenty feet away.' Grandmother took another very deep breath. She asked, 'Will we go hungry today if we don't eat that squirrel?' I knew we had just come home from town and had food for a week, so I said, 'No.' And she said, 'So you killed that squirrel for pleasure.' At this point, I knew I was in deep trouble. My brain was scrambling for some justification – was it going to bite someone, or hurt someone? Nothing came to my mind. She could tell I was searching for some reason to kill the squirrel, and she said, 'Lona, if you lie to me, it will hurt my heart. Be very careful right now.'

"I told her I wanted to show the other boys how good I am with the slingshot. She pointed out I could accomplish that by hitting targets and that the squirrel died for my pleasure. It died to make me feel big or better than others. Then she said, 'I understand wanting to be better at your age. All kids want that. But this animal died. It is a female. It will not return to its nest; it will not feed its babies.'

"By that time, I was crying. I felt like I didn't deserve to live, that I was evil. Grandmother came and stood over me and her face wasn't so stormy when I finally looked up. 'Do I need to go to the sweat lodge'? I asked. 'Do I need to do chores? Do I need to be spanked?

"'Lona, have I ever spanked you?' she asked.

'No, but I wish you would now.'

"She told me that would be too easy. She said she would show me how to repair this and to help my soul get fixed. 'I will show you how to skin and cook this squirrel in case you ever are hungry and need it for food, because that is the only reason we can take the life of a squirrel or rabbit. So now I will teach you how to cook this squirrel."

Lona smiled. "I, of course hated to cook, but we gathered onions and carrots from the garden, and other herbs and we simmered the squirrel with potatoes and some other root vegetables. It actually smelled really good and by the time we had finished, I found I liked cooking with Grandmother."

"So then you ate it?" Allie asked.

"No. We drove to a grandfather in her clan who lived alone, and his children did not care for him well. We went to his door with the stew and some fresh bread, and Grandmother asked him for a favor. She asked him for help in teaching me the lesson about why we can kill animals and if he had the time, to tell me one of the stories about greed. I remember his eyes got very big when he saw the pan of food and we sat with him as he ate it. I remember he had not had any food all day and he ate with such a delight."

"And the story he told you?" Allie asked.

"Who knows? I hardly ever listened to the elders telling stories of long ago with complicated names of dead people. But I do remember how important I felt that I had brought him food and he ate it with so much pleasure. After that I liked to feed others." Lona took a big bite of her sandwich.

"And did you get to eat any of the stew?"

"Oh no. And I didn't get to eat any dinner either. My grandmother wanted me to actually experience being hungry. I do remember that I ate her pancakes the next morning with butter and honey. I've never had as much pleasure eating pancakes since. The intensity of my hunger, my relief that my soul had been mended, and my relief that my grandmother still loved me. Whew, that was a powerful blend. It is one of my defining memories of my grandmother. It is something I can relive, not just remember."

Allie sat quietly next to Lona who seemed to linger in the memory. "Thank you for sharing that with me. I really like imagining the little tom-boy you were and the amazing grandmother you had."

Lona wiped a tear from her eye. "I haven't thought of that lesson for a long time. I needed to remember it. I haven't found many people to share my childhood stories with. Thank you for being a good listener." She squeezed Allie's hand, cleared her throat, "Let's eat the good food your mother prepared for us."

CHAPTER 16

Lona found herself somewhat subdued as they were approaching Allie's college town. She was still digesting her memory of her grandmother and managing her surprise that she had shared the memory with Allie. *This must be what the self-help book calls vulnerability. I don't especially like it, but I didn't die from it.*

"Do you like your college?" she asked Allie.

"I do. I don't have anything to compare it with, it is my only college experience. Despite my good grades, I was uncertain if we could afford me going to college. My dad was convinced we couldn't. My mom sort of snuck around him to get the money for me to take the kind of test you needed to apply to colleges. She and Aunt Marge and Matt and I drove to Charlottesville where the tests were given."

I think you mentioned this the morning after..." Her voice trailed off, and both of them shifted their bodies and Allie cleared her throat before continuing.

"Both mom and aunt Marge were tense on the drive there. And Matt and I were also anxious. I remember when we got our results, Matt and I were so relieved. We both did well enough to get accepted to several colleges."

"That sounds like she was really taking a risk to make sure you had a chance at college," Lona commented.

"Yeah, I was just so glad to go, that I haven't thought of how brave she was to do that. She rarely stood up directly to my father," Allie paused. "Hmm. Well, this is a weird memory of standing up. Mom used to do this one thing on April Fool's Day. Every year she would sneak into the bedroom and nail my dad's slippers to the floor. He'd get up in the morning and put them on and then fall. He never got hurt. They would both laugh and laugh. He'd never remember the night before April Fool's Day to check. She stopped of course once he got injured at work. He never made her stop and he never got angry about it."

"Wow," Lona exclaimed. "Remind me to never get into a practical joke competition with your mother. Allie, did you laugh when she'd do that?"

"I think I did. It just seemed normal to me. I guess not normal to other people." Allie paused. "Perhaps that was just her way of making peace with her year of compliance."

"What happened to your mom and Aunt Marge when the men found out about them helping you guys take the tests?"

"I don't remember. I think I was too worried about how to afford school. We still didn't have enough money to afford the room and board. But then I found out about Berea. There is no tuition for any of the students here, but you do have to work at least 10 hours per week, which helps pay for your room and board. Most kids graduate with zero loans or a very small debt."

"I didn't know that even existed," Lona said.,

"Well, all of us kids here are relatively poor, so we also get what are called Pell grants to help pay. But those are typically small and have low interest rates."

"What kind of work do you do at the college?" Lona asked.

"Every freshman must work either with the facility or with food service the first year. You learn how to be a good employee for which you get graded."

"I am impressed. What jobs have you had?

"I started with grounds maintenance and then got interested in all the sustainable farm programs. We manage 500 acres of pastures and crops and ponds and gardens, and 8000 acres of forest."

"No wonder you know so much about trees."

"There are other colleges and universities that operate sustainable farms, but we are rated number one in the United States," Allie proudly said.

"You're not going to believe this," Lona said, "But my grandmother went to the first Native American nursing school in the United States. It was in a town called Ganado on the Navajo reservation. It sounded a lot like your school. All the kids worked on the farm, on the grounds, and in the kitchen and cleaning. Back then nobody thought that the Indigenous People could ever be as smart as the white people. Grandmother said every woman in the graduating nursing classes passed the state nursing exams."

"Was this school run by the government?" Allie asked.

"No, those schools were brutal. Kids would essentially get

kidnapped or forced to go there. And punished if they ever spoke their native language. But this school had money from the Presbyterian church and while all the classes were taught in English and the kids had to learn to read and write in English, they were not punished for speaking their own language. And the parents who were nearby could visit and help the school survive, and they helped with the bigger building projects. They had some really committed teachers and staff."

"Is it still open?" Allie asked.

"Unfortunately, no. It kind of blows my mind that you now go to such a school."

"Yes, it started before the civil war and was the first school in the south to admit both African Americans and women. It, too, had very committed teachers and staff. When the politicians in the south made it illegal to have Blacks and Whites in the same schools, it almost closed."

"When did that happen?" Lona asked.

"Segregation in schools was always the standard in the south, even after the civil war. My school brought a lawsuit against Kentucky to allow desegregation, but it was denied by the Supreme Court in 1908. So Berea had to have separate buildings and classrooms and it basically shifted to just teaching poor white kids and the South could accept that. Then when the Supreme Court banned segregation in schools in 1954, our college opened back up to poor students, African Americans, White and Hispanic, and all others."

"You'll see when we get there. It is now very diverse. Except of course, we don't have very many rich kids. And no alcohol is allowed on campus, so we don't have very many drunk kids."

"That is interesting. My reservation doesn't allow the sale of liquor either. That is some story, and I can see why you are so proud of your school for taking a lead in that fight."

CHAPTER 17

They pulled off the highway and drove a short distance to the entrance of the college.

Allie pointed to a side street. "Let's park here outside the college for a moment. I'll show you the main entrance."

The sign marking the entrance was smaller than Lona would have expected: Two short brick walls straddled a walking path that led to an expansive park-like area filled with mature trees and crisscrossed with walking paths. Each brick wall ended in a modest brick column with a white capstone. The proportions of the wall and columns were pleasingly symmetrical. On the left wall, against a white background was the college name, BEREA, in a dark classic font. Across the path on the other wall was the word, COLLEGE. Through the entrance Lona could see various two-and three-story buildings, all of them constructed in the same brick, softened by window frames and doors of slightly cream color. One building that was particularly striking had two round columns going all the way to the high roof. The double door recessed entrance was shielded by a peaked gable. The main roof had a less severe peak and six cream-colored dormers decorated the roof above the two rows of six windows.

"The architecture here is called 'Georgian,'" Allie said. "Many of the colleges in the south have this style; it was popular in the mid to late 1800's."

"The whole effect is so filled with grace," Lona said. "It is both understated, and solid, and warm all at the same time."

"Oh, I am so glad you see that. This school is a refuge from so much in the world."

"Is your dorm one of these buildings?"

"No, my dorm is one of the newer ones just off the quad. Most of these buildings are classrooms and administration. But a couple of them have dorm rooms on the second floors. Let's get in the car and we can drive to my dorm and park behind it. It is finished in the same brick with cream trim, but the inside is more modern.

"Take this next road on the left. I thought we could stop at my dorm and unload my stuff and then we'll get some food and I'll give you a tour."

"That sounds good."

"There is some visitor parking around the back."

Lona pulled behind a three-story building. The windows and style were similar to the buildings on the Quad and she would never have guessed that it was newer construction. They grabbed all of Allie's stuff from the trunk and entered through a door in the back.

"We can take the elevator over here. I have my room on the top floor."

"Allie, this is very nice. Is it always this clean and well-kept?"

"Yes. Once you've been on the grounds or buildings staff, you tend to not litter. You realize someone has to pick up after you."

The elevator door opened onto a long hallway with doors leading off it into the individual rooms. Several doors were open and there was the chatter of students coming from the rooms. They walked past a lounge area situated in the middle of the floor, and a few kids were reading in some comfortable chairs or sprawled on sofas. Several of them called out "Hello" to Allie and she responded, but didn't stop and didn't introduce Lona. A few of the students seemed to watch Lona with curiosity as she followed Allie down the hall to her room. Allie opened the door.

"Here we are. As a senior, I finally got myself one of the few single rooms." Allie hurried to put her clothes and books away.

Lona stood in the doorway, looking at a single bed, well made with a bedspread that matched the curtains on the window. A small desk and bookshelves took up a corner and there was a comfortable chair on one side of the window overlooking the grounds beyond.

"Wow. This is very nice and homey."

"Yes. I love it. And I will miss it."

"Do you have your own bathroom?"

"No. Each wing has its' own bathroom and showers at the end of the hallway, and a kitchen that we can all share if we want to make some of our own food. It took a while for me to get used to sharing the bathroom, but everyone takes their stuff in a little bucket and your towel and just wait for an open shower. In fact, I need to use the bathroom now. Are you okay?"

"Yes. And you know, Allie, you and your mom did a good job with the makeup. The bruises are barely noticeable. I'll just wait here until you return."

Lona let herself wander to the window and admire the view. Then she returned to the bookshelf and read some of the book titles – mostly textbooks. She stopped at what had to be Allie's senior high school yearbook and pulled it down. She was still looking through it when Allie returned.

"Oh, dear: the yearbook," Allie said nervously.

"Yes. You seem to be on so many pages – band, chorus, Student Honor Society, cross country track team, language club, Student Council president? Oh, and this giant picture of you as the Citizenship/scholarship winner?"

"Ouch. Yes."

"Why, 'ouch'?"

"My friends tease me about the extent of my nerdiness," Allie replied.

"Not so many pictures in the scenes of parties," Lona commented, leafing through the book.

"Right. There you have it. Accomplished, but not exactly popular."

Lona paused. "Can I ask, why do you say you weren't popular?"

"Well, the lack of being at the parties, or on the Homecoming Court, or a cheerleader. Those were the popular girls who had lots of dates and boyfriends."

Lona was quiet, not sure what to say. Finally, she asked, "What did you do outside of all the school activities?"

"Church. My mom, the choir director at church, had us in the church youth group, remember?"

"I guess I didn't realize how much time that would take up."

"It wasn't just the time. It was the polarity between 'good girls and boys' and the party kids. Matt and I did not belong with the party kids. Preston did. But he and Matt had some connections because of sports." Allie sat in the chair by the window as Lona continued to look through the yearbook.

"Hey, here you are on the page for cross-country," Lona held out the picture for Allie to see. Allie took the book from her hands and placed it back on the shelf.

"Really? Don't you realize that cross country, by definition, is sort of a solo sport done in the woods? Sometimes we ran as a pack, but we were mostly breathless and did no talking."

Lona chuckled. "Okay. Yes, I guess there isn't much need to coordinate the running with others."

"The popular kids had the stress of having to be at the best parties and having the right dates. Matt and I by-passed all of that. Our parents kept us on a tight leash. And we were basically okay with that. We needed our time for schoolwork."

Again, Lona wasn't sure of what to say.

"How about you? Allie asked. Were you in the popular group?"

"Let me get to the bathroom and then perhaps we can eat

and then you can give me that tour."

Allie was beginning to wonder why Lona kept changing the subject whenever there was an inquiry about her parents or herself.

* * *

"Where to?" Lona asked as she started the car.

"I'll take you to the Farm Store. They have good sandwiches and amazing baked goods. It is casual, you okay with that?"

"I was born casual, remember? My people ate squirrels and bunnies."

"Well, none of those will be on the menu. But I think you will like it, nonetheless."

As Lona walked in the cottage-like building, she remarked, "Man, this place smells of cinnamon and baked bread."

"Right? It's like someone is always baking something good."

"Hey, Allie, did you have a good semester break?" the young woman behind the counter asked.

"Yes, and you, Claire?"

"Yeah, I finally got my research paper finished. Just got back last night."

"Great. Okay if we sit by the window and have some dinner?"

"Sure, take any seat. I'll bring some water and a menu, though you of course have it memorized."

"I can't help but notice that everyone here seems to know you," Lona said, sitting at the table.

"Right, it is like its own little town. And I have worked in this store or delivered produce here for four years."

Lona picked up her menu. "What do you like?"

"Claire," Allie called out, "I'll have the peanut butter, banana, honey on whole wheat with a side of fruit."

"And what for you?" Claire called out to Lona.

"The same," Lona replied.

Allie's eyes teared up again. "Ah, shit," she murmured. "I am so tired of this."

"Thoughts of Matt again?"

"No, my brother, Frankie."

"Oh, you have a brother?"

"Had. I had two brothers. Frankie died when I was seven. Jeff, my other brother, is two years older than me. Frankie was six years older."

Lona was silent for a while. "So, you're thinking of Frankie and his death now?"

"Yes. I followed Frankie around like a puppy, and whenever he asked for anything, I'd pipe up, 'the same.'"

"So when I called out 'the same' it triggered this memory of Frankie for you?" Lona said softly.

"Yeah. How's that for pathetic? I dealt with his death a long time ago." Allie swiped impatiently at her tears and Lona handed her a napkin.

Lona was again silent for a while as she waited for the tears to abate.

"Do you mind if I ask how he died?"

"It was some type of cancer. We knew he was in the hospital, but Jeff and I didn't know he was going to die. Mother just told me this past week that she never believed he was going to die. Even though the doctors had said his condition was serious, she just never believed it. I think she was trying to help me with the suddenness of Matt dying. Strange. She never told me that about Frankie before. In fact, no one in my family ever really talked about Frankie. I mean, we have this picture of him, but no one ever talks about him."

"Well, no wonder he is on your mind now. Lots of similar triggers," Lona suggested.

"Hmm. Yeah. I guess so. I never got to say good-by to either of them." Allie started to cry again.

Lona reached over and gently massaged a shoulder. "It is easier if you don't tighten up so much in your shoulders and throat."

"That is how I get these stupid tears to stop," Allie choked out.

"Yeah, I know. I spent a lot of time teaching myself how to not cry. I actually had to watch sad movies to learn how to cry again. I was so successful in shutting my tears off.

"And the self-help book says that when we need to cry, we should not fight it as much. It kind of says the problem isn't that bad things happened to us, but that we memorized a limited way of managing our pain."

"That is such bull-shit," Allie mumbled, but she tried to relax her shoulders and the spigot opened more. Now she was embarrassed that Claire would come over, which, of course, she did.

"Umm, Allie, are you all right?" Claire asked.

Allie tightened up again, and she couldn't get any words out.

"Thank you, Claire, for your concern. Allie just had some difficult family experiences over the semester break," Lona offered as an explanation.

Claire stood nervously by. "Allie, if you ever want to talk about any of this, you know, I'm always available."

"Thank you, Claire. I know you are. I think the food will help me," Allie managed to eke out.

"Coming right up." Claire hurried away.

"See?" Allie said. "This is what happens when you cry."

"Yes. It is." Lona just let the silence remain as Allie managed to stop the tears.

'It is damn inconvenient," Allie said with some frustration in her voice, as she blew her nose into the napkin.

"Yes, it is inconvenient."

The food arrived and they both started to eat.

"Damn, this is really good," Lona exclaimed with her mouth full. "Why have I never thought of this combination?"

"Perhaps just a lack of culinary imagination," Allie ventured.

Lona smiled. "Indeed. My people never put squirrels and peanut butter together."

They both relaxed and enjoyed the food.

When Claire returned with the check, they both reached for it. Each had one half of it in their hands.

"Don't make me hurt you," Lona said with a smile.

"Who says you could?" Allie replied.

"Okay, fair enough. How about, I have a job and you are a student."

"Yes, but I told you I also have a job, here. All of us do." They both continued to hold the check fiercely.

"Were you also on the debate team in high school?" Lona asked.

"No, but I am known far and wide for being competitive."

"That seems evident. Okay. Let's do this. Are there games somewhere on the campus? Like at an Activities Center?"

Allie's eyes lit up. "Of course, there are. I am particularly good at some of them. But we don't actually have an Activities Center. The games are scattered around in the dorms."

"So you pick the first game, I will pick the second and if we are at a tie, you get to pick the third game. Winner pays the check."

"You are so on." Allie said getting up to leave and releasing the check to Lona to pay.

As they were walking out the door, Lona asked, "How do you want me to handle any questions about how we know each other? What do your friends know?"

"Nothing. The police told me I can't talk to other people, only my family about this."

"Let's take a walk," Lona said directing them down the path bordering the lawn. "Allie, I think the police meant they didn't want you to talk to any people in town or any reporters because if there is a trial, they would have to excuse anyone from the jury you had spoken to, or who had formed any opinion about this."

"Oh. So I could share something with people here?"

"I think so, if you trust the people to not go talk to a reporter."

"But again," Allie persisted, "When I talk about it, I feel ashamed about crying, and I think people will judge me."

"Have you ever felt like I was judging you?" Lona asked.

"I guess I worry about it in the moment. But, no, I haven't felt like you judge me. So now, I am crying around you all the time."

Lona stopped walking and turned towards Allie. "Did you judge me when I told you about my grandmother, and I was tearful?"

"No, but you weren't all slobbery and out of control with your crying. Your crying was sort of contained and, and touching."

Lona took another deep breath.

"And could you please stop it with the deep breathing? I am starting to get that my crying is annoying to you."

Lona laughed out loud. "I'm sorry. It is just that, umm, I didn't know crying was yet another competitive action, you know, good versus bad crying. I remember saying to my therapist once, 'Do you get off on my crying?'" Lona continued to laugh.

"Okay, what?!!! You had a therapist?" Allie exclaimed.

"Of course I did. Do you think a twelve-year-old is going to lose the only mother and grandmother she has ever known and go from squirrels to Washington DC high cuisine and designer-clothed white girls – who, by the way, were very mean – and NOT need a therapist?! And this isn't some competition for who had the worst childhood. Allie, I like you. And I want to help you. And I think I have had some experiences I can share that will help."

"You like me?"

"Yes. I don't mean in a creepy way, like you. I just feel care and concern for you, and I think you are smart and talented and have a sense of humor. And, frankly, as I try to help you, I keep getting more insight into what I went through. And I think you are a really good listener, and you suck when it is your turn to share. At least to share with the other kids here."

"And what would I tell them? My cousin Matt was killed on the camping trip we went on, and the killer tried to rape me, and I nearly died, and the son-of-a-bitch still hasn't been arrested and he keeps telling others that maybe I killed Matt. And maybe I will have to stand trial or at least testify, and people may not believe me, and he will get away with it!!"

"I notice you are not crying now," Lona observed in a careful way.

"Do you want me to?" Allie said still with some defensiveness.

"No, but sometimes our anger is also a helpful tool when we have been through what you've been through."

"Well, which is it then, cry or rage.?" Allie almost stomped her foot as she demanded an answer.

Lona took a step backwards and forced herself to not take a deep breath. "All I know is that when really bad things happen, we tend to use ice or rage. I overused rage in my situation. Then I went to ice and numbness and keeping a lot of distance from others. I don't know, Allie, but I think we need some of all those things – ice, rage, and lately, I've been thinking that crying helps to not get stuck in ice or rage.

"So," Lona continued, "Perhaps you could tell some trusted people that Matt was killed on the camping trip and the police are still investigating the murder."

Allie seemed to consider this. "Okay, I guess that could work."

"And, Allie, if they ask how you met me?"

"I could say, shut up and mind your own business."

Lona laughed. "There you go, use a bit of the rage...or, perhaps you could say that I was a part of the investigation and now I am becoming your friend and just trying to help you."

"Are you becoming my friend?" Allie asked.

"I hope so. I would be honored to have you as a friend. Do you have an opening on your friendship list for me?"

"Let's see if you are a good loser, and then I'll consider it," Allie replied, having regained some of her composure.

"Oh, girl, you are so going down. And I like your cockiness. But tonight, in your house, on your court you are going down."

CHAPTER 18

Lona parked the car in the visitor parking lot closest to a dorm near Allie's. "I keep seeing some students with shirts that say 'One Blood.' What is that about?" Lona asked.

"That is our school motto," Allie replied.

"Hmm. It kind of sounds aggressive: One blood?"

"One of the early founders used the phrase: God has made of one blood all peoples of the Earth," Allie explained. "You know, that we are all equal, all the same."

"Hmm. So you guys couldn't just go with 'The Bull Dogs'?" Lona smiled. "You had to go with this whole equality thing in the confederate South? Frankly, it seems a little provocative."

"Right? We hope it is. We are kind of committed to radical acceptance," Allie replied with a touch of pride. "Turn in here, this dorm has the better games and tables."

Lona parked the car and then reached to keep Allie from getting out. "Allie, do I look okay for this activity?"

Allie was stunned. "Of course you do. Have you never been on a campus before?"

"Not until I came here with you."

"Well, everyone will sort of be dressed like us – casual, jeans, sweatshirts…actually, you are a little more put-together than most of us. Your blouse is tucked in, and your ankle boots and faded jeans are clean, hair combed, let me check your fingernails." She reached over and playfully took Lona's hand in hers to check her nails.

"Lona, your hands are really cold. What is going on?"

Lona pulled her hand away from Allie's warm one. "Actually, I am a little anxious. Okay, perhaps more than a little. Let's just say I had a difficult transition from the Rez to a private school in DC. I did not fit in, and I have some, uh, I guess exaggerated fear about being around people who are more educated..."

"And white?" Allie broke in.

"Yeah, I suppose, and white. I mean if you get bitten by a white dog, all white dogs make you kind of scared."

"Did the white girls bite you?"

Lona smiled. "Actually, um, one of them did. But we are not going down that road tonight."

"Well," Allie said. "Tonight, I've got your back and none of my friends are biters. I think they will be charmed by you. They will, of course, root for me because it is 'our house', as you would say. But in my house, my friend is safe."

Lona took a deep breath and opened the door, "Okay, let's do this." She let Allie lead the way.

As they entered the dorm, Lona saw a couch and some stuffed chairs. Off to the right were the usual active games: foosball and a pool table. Directly in front were more couches and chairs and some coffee tables.

Allie led the way to the foosball table. "Hey, Jake, Sam, can

I play the winner? This is my friend, Lona, and we have a bet riding on a foosball challenge."

"Hey, Allie," Jake responded. Sam nodded a hello. "Welcome back. Nice to meet you, Lona. I hope you know Allie has a reputation with her foosball skills."

"Please, Jake, I want to create shock and awe. I can't do that if you tip her off."

"Oops, my bad," he responded. "Good luck, Lona. Whatever you do, don't challenge her to a foot race. She's our resident rabbit. We are actually just finishing. Allie, do you have any money bet on this game?"

"Sort of. We have a bet regarding the check for our dinner. The bet involves two or three games. I pick the first game, Lona picks the second…"

"Which I now know will NOT be a foot race," interrupted Lona.

Allie gave a slight punch to Jake's arm. And I pick the third contest if one is needed," Allie said.

"Normally, Lona," Jake continued, "I would ask if you were available for any side bets, but I shall exercise some caution and see how the first game goes."

Jake and Sam stepped away from the table. Lona found herself liking the slightly teasing camaraderie and started to relax. "This feels like being in the rec center on the base," she whispered to Allie.

Lona took the handles on one side and Allie took the other ones. "As the visitor, shall I start?" Lona said as she placed the ball next to her defender bar.

"Okay and we will do best of three games?" Allie asked.

Lona nodded and executed a quick wall pass and put the first goal in with a push shot from the middle.

The next time Lona got the ball, Allie was blocking the wall pass, and she got control of the ball and made two goals of her own. The goals see-sawed back and forth in the first game until Allie started sneaking in pull shots and then a wicked fast snake shot to take a comfortable lead and win the first game.

Both women were grimly focused, and Lona squeezed out the second game through a combination of fast reflexes and luck. By the start of the third game a small crowd of the other students gathered to watch the intense battle. They cheered and moaned at the appropriate times, being appreciative of the good play by both women.

Lona knew she was outmatched. Allie had a variety of set plays and Lona's defense could only carry her so far. She saw how Allie was able to focus and defend against her own more limited strategies. Allie had more variety to her plays and much better technique. By the third game, Allie pulled into the lead and held it to the end.

"Don't feel bad, Lona," Jake said. "She beats all of us. At least you got one game. Most of us never get that."

"Thanks, Jake." Lona looked over at the pool table. "I choose pool for our next contest." *God help me. I hope she isn't a savant at pool also.* She started to rack the balls and then went to the other end of the table. "Loser breaks?" she asked of Allie.

"Sure. No problem. I'm just going to bask a little longer in my previous victory."

"You know, Allie, I would find you insufferable if I didn't know that you are going to lose in my game."

Lona had made a very tight rack of the fifteen balls and had chosen the better of the pool cues for herself. She unbuttoned the second button of her white blouse and rolled up her sleeves exposing the smooth skin covering her well-developed forearms. When she broke, the loud crack of the cue ball hitting the first ball of the tight triangle got the attention of the room. Heads turned and even more kids came over to watch the competition. Much of the talking got quieter in the room.

Lona was accustomed to that reaction when she broke, and the balls shot across the table. She had used her strong break and her gender to win money from many opponents. One of the solids dropped on the break and the balls were so evenly distributed by the force of the break that she could plot out her next four shots.

"I'll take the solids." She leaned down low over the cue ball sighting the path she wanted the next ball to take. The audience had to move away from her, and they instinctively lined up opposite so they could face her and get a good look down the shirt that she had unbuttoned. They got an enticing glimpse of her cleavage and the top lace of her bra. Allie moved with the audience and watched Lona calmly and efficiently run four more balls into the pockets before she finally ran out of balls she could drop.

"Your turn," Lona said as she chalked her pool cue and stood aside.

Allie had all seven of her balls on the table. *Well at least they aren't clumped together, and I see three that I think I can make.* She also moved easily around the table and put the three into the pockets. Then she went on the defense and left the cue ball trapped behind some of her other balls so that Lona did not have any clean shot.

Lona looked at Allie and smiled. "Nice leave." She slowly circled the table and then leaned down over the cue ball. "Number five in the side pocket," she said as she gave a small smile at Allie and then winked at her. She bounced the cue ball off two sides of the table and clipped the ball on its edge and dropped it. She left the cue ball in good position for the last ball. "Number eight in the end pocket." She popped it into the pocket with more force than necessary to punctuate the end of the game. The crowd erupted in cheers and whistles. She looked over at Allie whose mouth was open. She walked over to her.

"Allie, are you alright? We are even. What is next, you choose."

"I'm okay," Allie replied. "But I do need to use the rest room." She hurried away, and Lona found herself practicing being gracious to the students who wanted to know more about her and her pool skills.

Allie went into a stall in the rest room and sat down. *What is going on? Lona, she, she winked at me and my body is hot and my heart is racing. Get a grip! My body is doing that thing it does when I am around her. Actually, it is doing more than its usual thing. SHIT. I am getting turned on. I'm sure she doesn't mean to be doing that, but jeez. Everyone in the room is getting turned on, I bet. It's like, like if Brad Pitt were playing pool, or J-Lo, or Beyonce.* She took some deeper breaths to steady herself. *Okay, right. Everyone is kind of turned on. So this doesn't mean anything bad about me. At least I'm not having sexual feelings for a bear. I'm just like everyone else. Okay.* She let out a deep breath. *Let's go do this.*

She splashed some cold water on her face and thought about what the next challenge would be. She walked out of the rest room with a smile fixed on her face.

"So, we are tied." Lona stated. "What is the next challenge? Arm Wrestling?"

"Karaoke," Allie announced.

"What? No way. No fair," Lona exclaimed anxiously.

"It is fair. I get to choose. We have it all set up in the next room over by the wall. We have all kinds of music: country, classics, rock'n roll. We each pick one song and we'll get five of the students to be the judges."

The evening had turned from a two-person contest into a spectator event for twenty or so students and when they heard Allie's proposal, there was considerable encouragement and excitement. Clearly, karaoke was a college sport here. Several hands were going up of students who wanted to be judges. Allie chose five.

Lona was having a battle with her anxiety. "I tend to do my singing alone in cars or showers. I have never performed in front of others," she said, hoping to talk Allie out of this challenge.

"You said I get to pick the last game, and this is it, but if you just want to forfeit the win to me, you can do that."

Lona felt twenty sets of eyes on her. She thought to herself, these are nice kids. Not a mean one in the bunch. She could hear them saying encouraging words. She let herself join the group as they moved towards the end of the room. There was a piano next to the wall and some guitars and percussion instruments scattered about. "No way do I want to forfeit, but I don't know how to work this equipment."

Allie walked over to a black box with a microphone plugged into it. "See, you type in a song or a performer and it gives you all these options and then you hit play and start to sing. The lyrics appear on the screen over there."

"Are there some group songs, like with back-up singers?" Lona asked.

"Sure," Allie said and several of the students, male and female offered to help and be back up if she needed them. "We do this all the time, Lona. It is really fun, and I've heard you sing and you have a nice voice," Allie said encouragingly.

Lona started typing and then waved several of the females and Jake and Sam over to huddle with her. They broke from the huddle and the back-up singers arranged themselves in a half circle behind Lona. The judges had settled themselves in five chairs, each with a pad of paper and pencil. The others stood back and gave Lona and her group some room. Lona found herself looking towards the far wall as she fingered the bear on her necklace and asked for courage. Then she hit the play button.

Lona pictured herself in her own room dancing and singing and pretending she was Meghan Trainer singing, *IT'S ALL ABOUT THE BASS, 'BOUT THE BASS, NO TREBLE.*

Lona and all the young people had memorized the video of Meghan and her hit song and could easily do the steps and hand movements. As the song progressed all of them became more relaxed and more bawdy in their dancing and thrusting of their top and bottom parts. Jake and Sam were particularly entertaining as they mimicked the young women. By the end of the song, there was much laughter, and it was hard to tell who were the back-ups and who was in the audience. Lona found herself relaxing into the fun of the song and she sold it. At the end there was raucous applause.

The judges were generous – all fours and fives.

Lona motioned Allie onto the makeshift stage. Several kids called out suggestions to Allie. Clearly, Lona thought, Allie has done this before.

"I have been working on a more recent Trainer song," Allie said. "It's a little more risqué and doesn't lend itself as much to a group performance. But since Lona was such a good sport, here goes." She hit the play button.

I COULD HAVE MY GUCCI ON
I COULD WEAR MY LOUIS VUITTON
BUT EVEN WITH NOTHIN' ON
BET I MADE YOU LOOK (I MADE YOU LOOK)...

This was certainly a side of Allie Lona had never expected. She stopped thinking of her as an innocent girl and considered her to be a provocative woman. The rest of the audience seemed to be having a similar experience. There was no heckling or singing along. Lona watched Allie look directly into the eyes of the other students and tease and control the room with the song. Lona found herself getting turned on as Allie sang. *Shit, I do not want to be having these feelings.* She tried to look away but her eyes were glued to Allie. Her eyes were too happy watching her.

At the end of the song, there was a hushed silence and then a loud exhale and applause. There was no question, the judges gave all fives.

Lona and Allie approached each other and hugged. Great job, they each whispered. Both felt relieved and happy. Allie stuck a twenty-dollar bill in Lona's pocket. "I don't know when I have enjoyed losing so much as tonight," Lona said.

"Best win of my life," Allie replied.

"Hey, Allie, we need to practice for the graduation song. Play the piano for us, we'll just go through it a couple of times."

"Yeah," several of the others chimed in.

"I'll conduct and choose each student who may need to add their own verse," Jake piped up.

It seemed to Lona that the group didn't want to have the fun of the evening stop and that perhaps the song was like some last song done at the end of a concert.

"Lona, do you mind staying for just this one more song?" Allie asked. "It is sort of our school song, and we use it for bonding. And for encouragement."

"Sure. No hurry."

Allie sat down. "Okay here we go." She hit some chords on

the piano and the entire room started to stomp their feet in unison to provide the noise of marching as they sang:

AIN'T GONNA LET NOBODY TURN ME 'ROUND
TURN ME 'ROUND, TURN ME 'ROUND
AIN'T GONNA LET NOBODY TURN ME 'ROUND
I'M GONNA KEEP ON WALKIN'
KEEP ON TALKIN'
MARCHIN' UP TO FREEDOM LAND
AIN'T GONNA LET INJUSTICE TURN ME 'ROUND
TURN ME 'ROUND, TURN ME 'ROUND
AIN'T GONNA LET INJUSTICE TURN ME 'ROUND
I'M GONNA KEEP ON WALKIN', KEEP ON TALKIN'
MARCHIN' UP TO FREEDOM LAND

Jake turned and pointed to a young woman with her hand raised, and she sang out:

AIN'T GONNA LET A BAD BOYFRIEND
TURN ME 'ROUND
TURN ME 'ROUND, TURN ME 'ROUND
AIN'T GONNA LET A BAD BOYFRIEND
TURN ME 'ROUND
I'M GONNA KEEP ON MARCHIN' KEEP ON WALKIN'
MARCHIN' UP TO FREEDOM LAND

Jake pointed to another raised hand and a boy sang out:

AIN'T GONNA LET NO CHEMISTRY TEST
TURN ME 'ROUND
TURN ME 'ROUND, TURN ME 'ROUND
AIN'T GONNA LET NO CHEMISTRY TEST
TURN ME 'ROUND

I'M GONNA KEEP ON MARCHIN' KEEP ON WALKIN'
MARCHIN' UP TO FREEDOM LAND

Lona was realizing the song was being used for individual students to state their challenge and to get the support of the group to encourage them. She noticed that Allie's playing was getting softer and Allie raised her hand and Jake nodded to her:

AIN'T GONNA LET COUSIN'S MURDER
TURN ME 'ROUND
TURN ME 'ROUND, TURN ME 'ROUND
AIN'T GONNA LET COUSIN'S MURDER
TURN ME ROUND

Allie's voice choked as the group of kids surrounded her and held her and each other as they sang without the piano:

I'M GONNA KEEP ON MARCHIN', KEEP ON WALKIN'
MARCHIN' UP TO FREEDOM LAND

There were no further verses as Allie cried, surrounded by her classmates and friends who held her. Some of them crying with her.

Lona felt her throat tighten and her breathing get more shallow. She moved towards the exit and felt like she had to get outside or collapse. She was overcome with her own sadness and loneliness. The support being shown to Allie broke through every wall she had carefully erected for herself. She fled to her car and gave in to the tears that overwhelmed her. When her hands stopped shaking, she texted Allie that she hoped she would let the love and support just flow into her. She explained that she needed to be at work in the morning and would call her tomorrow when she got the chance.

CHAPTER 19

Lona pulled up outside her cottage. *Man, I am tired. And also, kind of lighter. That crying stuff really takes it out of me.* She opened the door to her room and switched on the overhead light. She gasped. Someone had been in her room and spray painted her bedspread. Her clothes were tossed about her room, the drawers were pulled out from her bureau and scattered on the floor. She stood silently listening and reached for a bully stick she kept just inside the door frame. She moved quietly to check the bathroom to make sure the intruder was no longer present. Returning to her bed she saw black letters unevenly scrawled across the blanket. GO BACK WHERE YOU BELONG. She saw the screen on the open side window was off, but the glass wasn't broken.

The heat of rage flared into her followed quickly by an icy calm as she shifted into her police role. She grabbed the flashlight she kept by her bed and went outside the window. There were no footprints under the window. Someone had raked the dirt and continued with their raking away from the house. The raked trail ended at the edge of the pavement on the access road. *If they were careful enough to rake, I suspect they also wore gloves. Damn TV shows instruct everyone how to avoid being caught. I'll give this a better look tomorrow morning. Did he know I was going to be gone? Another leak of information? A long list of people who knew I would be out of town. All of Allie's family and the police. And Jim and Chuck. Some employees who were covering for me. Shit. I assume this isn't random. This must be related to the case.*

She returned to the room and took pictures of the damage. She considered calling the crime scene people but decided instead to just clean everything up. She was glad she had taken her phone and laptop with her. She checked and what small amount of casual jewelry she owned was all there. As she was putting her clothing and underwear back into the drawers, she noticed her favorite bra and matching panties were gone. *Hmm. Well that was a rookie mistake. Clearly no value in taking that to a pawn shop. Nope. That was stupid.*

She finally fell into a restless sleep shortly before dawn.

* * *

The next morning Lona searched for any trail left by the intruder, but the asphalt driveway held no clues. There were no tire tracks. She assumed he had used the public parking lot outside the entrance gate and walked to her cottage. There were no surveillance cameras in the park and no other nearby employees to question. She knew Jim had arranged for someone to cover her early morning shift. She went in search of him and found him in the maintenance shed. He was checking the inventory of the supplies needed in the Park.

"Hey Lona, I thought you'd be sleeping in this morning," He continued to put supplies on the shelf.. "Did you get Allie safely to school?"

"I did, and I got to meet some of her friends and see the campus. I think she will be receiving a lot of support there for what she went through," She paused and moved around so she could face him. "I had hoped to sleep in, but someone vandalized my place." She held up her phone to show him the pictures she had taken.

"What?" He reached for her phone.

"You can just swipe to the right."

"Oh, Lona. Who would do that?" He scrolled slowly through all the pictures, his surprise replaced by anger. Oh, Lona, I am so sorry you had to return to this, and I can't believe anyone in our park would do this. Do you think it is related to Allie's case?"

"That is my first assumption," Lona replied. "But have you heard any negative gossip about me from any of the employees here?"

"Hmm. I haven't heard anything negative. A couple of the guys who deliver supplies saw you and asked about you about a month ago. They made some comment about how awful it would be for me to work with you. It was about you being attractive. I know these guys and it was typical guy stuff, nothing about your not belonging. Nothing registered as creepy to me. And the volunteers and staff here tend to be good people.

I know that sounds biased, but bigots don't last here very long. I won't have it."

Lona believed him. "Yeah, that has been my experience with all the people who work here."

Jim continued looking at the pictures. "I'm just thinking out loud here, but they had to have brought the paint with them. So, it was premeditated. They wanted to send a message. I don't see anything broken. Obviously, there isn't much in your room to break. Just the bedspread destroyed. This may sound weird, but I don't get a feeling overall of rage here. I am outraged, but I am not sure the vandal was. More like, someone sent to do a job. To deliver the message." Jim paused. "Of course, all of that is just my speculation. What do you think?"

"Well, I've been thinking about this all night. Who wants me gone? Who would benefit if I am not around?"

"You are the only witness to Allie's statements," Jim interjected.

"Not the only one," Lona replied. "The police have her report, the hospital has its pictures."

"You are the only non-local witness," Jim said.

Lona's stomach tightened in a familiar way. "Yep, outsider is my middle name here." Lona paused and decided to trust Jim. "I think someone is leaking information to Preston or his family, so I am going to be more careful about letting people know my comings and goings. I want your help in keeping my scheduled absences as private as possible."

"Of course, I can do that. Do you need better locks? He asked.

"No, they came in through the screen on a window that I had left open. Which I won't do again. And they were careful to not leave any footprints outside the window. And I am sure they would have worn gloves."

"Do you want to report this to the county sheriff or do you want me to?" Jim asked.

"I will let Chuck know but I don't want to bother them with investigating the vandalism when I know they will find no usable evidence. If there is another incident, then I'll have them open a case."

"Okay. But I still want to put a better lock on the front door," Jim replied. "And you can borrow our car if you are going to be away from the cottage, if that will help."

"That is so generous. For a while, I am going to be extra careful to be in the cottage at a reasonable time. Just leave the extra door lock for me and I can put it on this evening. I think it is the 'advance notice' that is the problem. I suspect the leak is coming from outside the park."

"Do you need an extra blanket? Yours is ruined now. Dammit. I assume there is no way to remove the paint."

"I agree. Thankfully, it isn't a genuine antique, not a four-point blanket purchased with Beaver skins at a trading post," Lona said with a smile. "I can order a replacement from the internet and have it delivered to the office."

CHAPTER 20

Lona finished checking in the campers and turned to Jim. "Do you mind if I take some time to make some phone calls?"

"Sure. The evening check-in seems over. Have any results come back from all the evidence they collected?"

"No, probably another week. But I'm not hopeful."

"Hope seems hard to hold onto these days."

"Yep." Lona walked into the back office and called her father. He picked up on the second ring.

"Hey Lona, is everything okay?"

"Hey, Dad, yes. Is this a convenient time for me to reach you?"

"Sure, let me just close the door. What's up?"

"I have met a young woman who will be graduating Berea College this June. She has a double major in Agriculture and Marketing. She is wicked smart and a very hard worker and has a good personality and works well with others."

"This is starting like a reference letter," he mused.

"Yes, I guess it is. I know she would be a good hire for the Department of the Interior if there are any internships that have become vacant or even an entry level job. I don't know who to have her send a job application to, but if you could be on the look-out for her inquiry and forward it to the right place, I would appreciate it."

"Lona, you have never asked me for anything like this before, or actually, never asked me for, like, any favors. I am kind of happy to hear a request. And, I need to ask, is she special to you in some way?"

"She doesn't have any family to help her with the college to work transition. And no private networking for herself…And yes, she is special to me. She had some trauma that occurred here in the Park, and we got close and we are working on a friendship."

"Well, okay then. Thank you for asking for some help. Have her download an application from the federal government website and have her email her application to my email address. What is her name?"

"Allie Cooper. Do you think there might be some openings?"

"Nothing at the higher pay grades of course. But if she is willing to start at the bottom, I can certainly find her a place. We often get last minute openings even if some are on projects that are temporary. Any chance I can wrangle a visit from you to go along with this favor?" "Dad, I know I have not been very available for a long time. I hope to make some changes with that. I do want to have a dinner or visit with you soon, and I hope we can include your girlfriend. Let me see when I have a couple of days off and I'll text you the dates to see if it works for your schedule."

"That sounds great. How is your new job going?"

"Well, I really like my boss and I like the trees."

"And the public relations part?" he asked.

"Ah, Dad. I still feel like I'm not sure what I want to be when I grow up."

"Lona, please consider the dinner. I think I have become a better listener."

"Thanks, Dad. I am working on becoming a better talker. Umm ... I, I have been missing you. I haven't given you much to listen to in a long time. I want to work on that.

"Hmm... I miss you too, honey."

Lona heard him clear his throat as she cleared hers. "Okay. Talk to you later, Bye."

"Bye, Lona."

Lona hung up. Her heart was racing. *Jeez. Why am I still so anxious talking to my dad? Perhaps, just a lack of practice? The book says to commit to some actions even if I am anxious. Well, today was a good example of that.*

Lona called Allie.

"Lona, you left so quick last night. Why didn't you say good-by?"

"Didn't you get my text?"

"I did, but, oh, never mind."

The silence hung between them.

"Allie, I know I left abruptly. And I had a very good time with you and your friends. Hell, the entire experience of being at Berea was great. But when I saw how much support and caring you were receiving from your friends at the end, it triggered some painful memories for me, and I just had to leave."

"Oh, Lona. I am so sorry."

"No, don't be sorry. It is helping me, I hope, to do some useful change in my life. How are you managing having told everyone about Matt's death?"

"Well, once I opened the spigot, it all came out. The attempted rape, the trial. All of it. You wouldn't believe how many of my friends have had similar trauma. They have been so supportive. They have signed up for sleeping in my room with me, one at a time, so I am not left alone. They wake me if I'm having a nightmare, and they made me sign up to see the counselor here. I have an appointment with her tomorrow."

"You've been having nightmares? You didn't tell me that."

"Yeah, I think maybe you and I don't tend to volunteer information about, you know, emotional stuff."

"Hmm. Well, I want to get better at that," Lona replied.

"Lona, are you feeling better, now?"

"Actually, yeah. I am. I did the crying thing on the way back, and I've been at work and functioning. Sometimes, I don't realize how closed off I have become."

"Right?! I didn't realize how much distance I was keeping from the kids here until this," Allie responded.

"Speaking of distance, I called my dad just now. You know, I told you he works in the Department of the Interior. He is quite a bit more than the janitor. Actually, he is a pretty big Poo-Bah. I told him that you are graduating and that I think you would be a good person to hire because of all your knowledge of farming and forests and other good qualities. I didn't tell him of the circumstances of your trauma. Anyway, I will give you his email address. You can download the application from the federal government web site, and once you fill it out, send it to him directly, and he will find a job for you somewhere. Allie, I am pretty sure you can get a job after you graduate, and I think you might like helping the federal government do a better job of managing federal lands."

Lona heard Allie crying. She choked out, "Happy, happy tears." She collected herself and continued, "I can't thank you enough. I have been so lost about the next step. You know I could begin at the janitor position."

"I know you could, but I think once he sees your grades and work experience at Berea, he will put you into a place that has more upward mobility.

"The good thing is that the Department is huge and once you have your foot in the door, you will have the time to direct yourself to the parts of the job that you like the most," Lona volunteered.

"It seems like I am having a lot of lessons in letting other people help me. It feels surprising and anxious. But I think I may get used to it, given enough time. Back to you, Lona. Are you feeling better?"

"I am now." She gave Allie her dad's email. "Let's try and talk every day, perhaps around 9:00 pm when our work is done?"

"I'd like that, Lona."

"Great, talk to you then later tonight?"

"Yep. Bye."

"Bye." Lona hung up. *I sure do enjoy helping Allie. If only I could make a job out of that. Perhaps I do need to talk to dad about my future. He probably knows a lot about that kind of stuff.* She felt her heart race again. *Okay, baby steps here.* But she did finish her work and locked up the office, glad that she hadn't shared about the break-in with everything else Allie was managing.

* * *

Allie's Dream

I am lost in a city. It is dark, not many streetlamps. I sense that someone is following me. I turn down streets and alleys trying to lose the follower. I am looking for an open store or anything with lights. I am looking for someone to help me. I hear the footsteps getting closer. Finally, I see a diner. The sign says OPEN ALL NIGHT. I run through the door looking for the night manager. I can't see her face, but she says she wants to hire me. I tell her I am being chased and she locks the door behind me. We start talking about wages and shifts and I wake up.

Lona's Dream

I am in a forest at night. I don't recognize anything. No idea where I am but I am following a faint trail, more an animal trail than a trail for people. I don't know where this trail leads, but I follow it. I squint my eyes to see better, and I notice a large, downed tree. It has been on the ground a long time. There is moss on it and several young trees have sprouted on its top side. It is a big log.

I hear a noise in front of me and I turn in that direction. I squint again and see a large black shape ahead of me on the trail. I follow it. I wake up.

CHAPTER 21

It is nine pm. Lona and Allie have been calling each other every night for two weeks, sharing their report of their days' events, and their feelings from the day.

"Hey, Lona. How was your day?"

"You know, the usual – wildly exciting six hours of checking in campers followed by a few hours of data input and cleaning campsites. But one family was particularly cute. It was a young couple with twin boys, perhaps ten years old. I may visit with them tomorrow and if the parents are okay with it, share my sling shot with them and see if they can beat me."

Allie laughed. "You are such a flirt with preadolescent kids."

"Indeed I am. I want to vaccinate all kids with doses of nature. And the parents had such good energy. Who knows, I might be able to wrangle a cup of hot chocolate out of these people if I play long enough with the kids. How are you doing, Allie, with your exams, your sleep, your dreams?"

"I am finally sleeping well enough that the sleep brigade is no longer on duty. They haven't had to wake me for a few days now. I sort of had a dream that normally might have awakened me, but it didn't. Want to hear it?

"Of course."

She proceeded to tell Lona of her dream about the diner.

"What do you make of the dream, Allie?"

"Well, it started like most of the nightmares. Dark place and being chased. But the geography of a city wasn't as frightening and then the diner thing. Perhaps that is related to my relief about the possibility of a job. I did get all my application material sent to your dad. He sent me a nice letter of encouragement and said he might have some possibilities within a couple of weeks. He seems nice, Lona."

Lona remained silent. She was lying on the replacement blanket that had arrived within days of the vandalism.

"Anyway, I took an exam today in research methodology and I think I got a good grade. Just two more to go. Why do you always ask me about my dreams?"

"My people think our souls and the souls of animals and other people visit us in our dreams. I grew up asking my family and friends about dreams, but I can stop it if it weirds you out."

"No, it doesn't. Sometimes after I have told you my dreams, I see them in a different light. And it helps me to see how they are becoming less frightening. How about you, any interesting dreams?"

"I had a good one last night." She proceeded to tell Allie of the dark woods, and the faint trail and the dark shadow.

"You weren't scared?"

"No. Just lost but not scared."

"The dark shadow didn't scare you. It sounds like a bear to me."

"I hope it was a bear. I think it was. Remember we think of animals as guides. When a bear is in my dream, I take it as a sign of my grandmother. I think I told you that her totem was a bear. And her last gift to me was her necklace with the bear carved from turquoise. She told me that she would always be watching out for me. So when I have a bear dream, I feel close to her, and safe. I wonder if the faint trail represents my questions about where I am going in my life. The path is not clear to me."

"So you may become an animal trainer?" Allie ventured.

Lona rewarded Allie with a chuckle. "Oh, gwasshopper you have a long way to go on your spiritual journey. I'm thinking of visiting my dad and talking to him about my career stuff."

"I am surprised you haven't talked to him about job stuff. He seems like he must have a lot of experience in that if he has worked so long for the government. Why haven't you asked him for help?"

There was a prolonged silence.

"Oops. I shouldn't have asked, right.?"

"No, you should have asked. It is a very logical question. I have such anxiety when it comes to my father. I have not spent time trying to figure it out. I just manage the anxiety by avoidance." Lona had started to pace as she talked.

"Does he live alone?"

He does, but he has a girlfriend and they both have their own places. They seem to me to be a committed couple."

"Do you like her?" Allie was propped up by pillows in her bed, enjoying their nightly chat.

"I think I might if I ever spent any time with her. My visits with my dad have been so infrequent that I think she stays away because she doesn't want to intrude on what little time we do have with each other."

"My therapist, Dr. Rivera, has been asking me quite a bit about my family and my brother's death," Allie responded. "I am sort of looking at why I treat them the way I do and, you know, perhaps why I haven't gotten very close to other people and, you know, not much dating or romance. Like maybe I didn't see marriage or closeness as a good thing."

"Wow. You guys are getting right down to it pretty quick," Lona responded.

"Right? I can't say I like it as much as foosball. She says we don't have much time with me graduating soon. So we are on the accelerated course of discovering that perhaps my childhood was worse than I thought."

Lona was at a loss for words.

"Anyway, I hope I can get some good sleep tonight. We've been living under the threat of a panty raid," Allie continued.

"I thought that went out with the old fraternity pranks," Lona interrupted. "Have you … umm, lost any underwear, Allie?" Lona inquired.

"No. there is just a lot of squealing and running up and down the halls. I think it is mostly kind of performative. But it is sometimes hard to underestimate the amount of energy that boys have for underwear acquisition."

Something clicked at the edge of Lona's memory.

"New topic," Allie said. "Graduation. Any chance you

would want to attend? My folks will be there and would like to see you again. They don't need you to drive. But your last visit caused you so much pain, and I don't want you to have to go through that again…What do you think?" Allie's heart was racing during the silence and she no longer felt relaxed. "Okay. Never mind, I shouldn't have asked you."

"Hold on. I just need to think about this."

"You're doing the breathing thing again, aren't you?"

Lona gave a nervous laugh. "You are getting spooky with how well you know me. I would rather be face-to-face in some of these harder conversations."

"Okay," Allie said. "Here goes. Just tell me if I am being too intrusive. I am wondering if your discomfort at Berea is related to the mean girls, the bite thing, the trauma that happened to you in school. And I am wondering if it would help you or us if you told me about it. Whew."

There was a prolonged silence.

"Lona? Are you there?" Allie asked, fidgeting, and twirling her hair.

"I haven't shared it with anyone except my old therapist, and I guess, with my dad. And that didn't turn out very well. So, I am quite nervous about it, and I do not want to do this over the phone."

"I can certainly relate to that. I have something I am afraid to share with anyone too. Maybe we could make a 'share date.'"

"Let me see if I can trade some shifts here. Do you have some free time during the week? It is hard to get away on the weekends," Lona said.

"I have more spare time than usual since we are at the end of the year, and I am caught up and don't have any major papers due. Monday or Tuesday next week would be good for me. We could go to some private place in the woods and talk."

"Sounds good. I'll text you tomorrow as to when I could get there."

"Okay. And thanks, Lona, for hanging in there with me."

"No, thank you, Allie, for hanging in with me."

"Good night."

"Good night."

* * *

Lona had been reading the book Mary had given her, searching for the answer on how to feel less anxious and more joy in life. As she was driving to Berea to meet with Allie and share some of her life history, she wanted to find a way to feel less anxious. *This friggin' book doesn't tell me how to not be afraid. In fact, The book wants me to tell myself and another person every crappy thing that happened to me, and, worse, every crappy thing that I did to others. Oh, and I am supposed to just let myself wallow in the suffering. Okay, that is my word. The book says I need to then be compassionate to myself and it will help me love myself. But there is no avoiding the shame and vulnerability. Yeah, that word is like a mantra to her. But she also says that I need to find a safe place and safe people if I am going to step into all those difficult feelings. Man, I hope that this doesn't totally blow Allie's fondness for me. I am so pathetic, wanting her to like me. I hope she is one of my safe people. Okay, just stop rehearsing what I am going to tell her. Turn on some music and then just go for it.*

She decided to call Chuck and tell him about the theft of her underwear.

"Hey, Lona, how are you doing?" Chuck answered his phone.

"I am hanging in there. Are you alone and do you have a minute? I wanted to get your thoughts on something. I didn't tell you that when my cottage got vandalized, I discovered that a matched pair of my panties and a bra were missing. I assume they were taken by the person who broke in and did the vandalism."

"And why are you telling me this now?" Chuck asked in a neutral voice.

"I think I withheld the information because it just felt too personal. And a little vulnerable," she paused. "But recently Allie mentioned that the women in her dorm were on the lookout for end of the year pantie raids. And I realized that adolescent boys are evidently notorious for wanting underwear. And then I thought it might be a helpful clue about the identity of the vandal. And I was wondering if it made sense to cross check the people who are most dependent on Preston's father for work and any record of sexual misdemeanors or families who have adolescent sons. I know that could be very time consuming. But perhaps if we narrow the search…"

her voice trailed off.

"I am sorry you felt vulnerable about that. And you are right, I think this adds a possible layer. I can't figure out a way to get a warrant for every adolescent in the county and look in their closets. But I can take a look at the list of employees or business interests of Preston's dad and see if anyone of them has any arrests or complaints of sexual misbehavior. We can just keep the vandalism case on our radar. We never actually opened a case because we didn't do any forensics on the cottage because it seemed such a dead end, evidence wise. I'll let you know what I come up with."

"Thanks, Chuck. I am sorry I didn't let you know about this earlier. I kind of behaved like a typical victim. I just shut down on that personal part. And the case with Matt and Allie seemed much more important."

"No worries. One step at a time here."

* * *

Allie and Lona were sitting under some large pine trees on top of a ridge that gave them a view of the valley below them. The hike had seemed effortless except for the dread that Lona wore like a heavy backpack.

"Lona, you know you don't have to tell me about this event. You are clearly burdened with it, and we can just skip this. I'm sorry I asked you to tell me." Allie reached for her water bottle and took a long drink.

“No, Allie. If I want to have a real relationship, then I have to do some talking that is uncomfortable for me. I have been reading more of that book in preparation, but it pretty much says the only way through this is to quit avoiding it. So, here goes. But I do need to sit further away from you. In fact, I need to stand up and just move a little as I talk. You stay seated.” Lona began to pace around the edge of the blanket in front of Allie.

“When I was thirteen, my father had enrolled me in this private school. I was lonely and the only person I could find to sit with at lunch was another misfit. Her name was Nancy Kim. She was from South Korea and her dad was part of their embassy staff in DC. We kept to the outskirts and were basically shunned by all the popular kids. The other less popular kids were already formed into their various cliques. But, thankfully, Kim hung in there with me. She was really smart, and she helped me with just about every subject. I was way behind academically.

“Her parents wanted her to make friends with kids who would be good contacts as she got older, but neither of us could find out how to break into the circle. Nancy was getting pressure from her parents to go to the fall dance at school. She begged me to go with her and I gave in. We got ourselves all dressed up and we had been practicing some of the popular dance moves. So, we go, and we hang at the edges of the dance floor and pretend we are cool. I could see that the cool kids were sneaking drinks from hidden flasks. We stuck to soda.

"Eventually Nancy said she had to go to the rest room. At that time, no girl ever went to the rest room alone. I went with her. When we entered, we saw a pack of the more popular girls taking up most of the space. One of them said in a slurred voice, 'Oh, look who's here, the Indian and the Slant Eye.'"

Allie gasped. Lona stopped her pacing and then resumed. "Anyway, Nancy moved back behind me and wanted to leave, but I wasn't going to let them stop us from using the toilet. There were four stalls and the door to the one furthest away was open, so I took Nancy's hand behind my back and tried to pull her behind me as I waded into the group blocking the way. They did not move, and my shoulder brushed the shoulder of the girl who was clearly inebriated. She made some noise like she had just been dirtied by something filthy. I said something like, 'Just move aside, we want to use the toilet'. She said something like, 'Wait outside.' And as I kept walking someone put out a foot and Nancy tripped, pushing me into Slurry Voice. And then someone pushed me into the toilet stall occupied by a girl pulling up her pants. Basically everyone was pushing and shoving now and I am trying to protect Nancy who is crouching down in all of this and getting shoved around.

"Somehow I get shoved into the empty stall and someone tried to pull my hair, but they got my grandmother's necklace instead and it flew off my neck into the toilet."

"Oh, Lona, no." Allie got up and went to Lona and took her hand. "And then what happened?' She asked quietly.

Lona had stopped pacing, and then she started to cry. "I don't know what happened next. Some of the girls told the police that I went crazy hitting them. Somehow, I got bit by someone. I don't remember anything after seeing the necklace in the filthy toilet. I don't remember reaching in to get it, but I did have it clenched in my hand when the police came in. I remember them coming in."

Lona was crying harder now. "I just went crazy. I don't remember." Her legs buckled and she knelt on the blanket. Allie slid down with her and positioned herself to be next to Lona. She held Lona as she cried, just making soothing noises and rocking her. Eventually, Lona's tears stopped, and she got control of her voice.

"What happened after the police came?" Allie asked.

"Well, Nancy stood up for me, but the other girls all told a similar version. And basically, I had gone crazy. Several of them had bruises on their faces. One girl had a black eye." Lona separated herself from Allie but continued to hold her hand.

"But Lona, this wasn't your fault."

"Well, I didn't start it. But seeing the pictures of the bruises… Allie, I scared myself. I thought I was crazy. I thought I would go to jail. I thought my dad would send me back somewhere. But I had nowhere to go back to." She cried again and Allie held her again.

"I wish I could have been there. I want to go break their legs," Allie said fiercely.

"Thank you. I would hate to see the damage if both of us had been there. I held on to my anger and blame for a long time, but the real damage was that I scared myself. I did think

I was crazy. Everything I had ever seen on TV was Indians and their crazy blood lust and torture of white people and I just felt like I had let my grandmother down and all of my people." Lona cried again. "You know, I never put it together that my shame was partly because of the stereotype of Indians. Hmm. That is interesting." She felt something loosening in her chest.

"Hmm. You don't think I'm crazy?" Lona asked, finally looking directly into Allie's eyes.

"God, no. I do want to go break their legs for how they hurt you."

Lona took some deep breaths and cleared her throat. "Hmm. My dad treated me differently after that incident. He got me out of the juvenile detention facility, and I got probation and had to go to counseling. And he enrolled me in a public school that was more diverse, and I was able to join some sports clubs and I didn't get in any more trouble. But I think I thought that he thought I was crazy. He got distant and worked a lot."

Allie let the silence lengthen. "This may not be right, Lona, but I wonder if he felt guilty about what happened. He was the one who put you in that school. Perhaps he dealt with his guilt by being distant."

Lona took a deep breath considering what Allie had said.

"Well, I never thought of that before." Lona felt some more sensations in her chest. "He was very reluctant to go to counseling with me. Hmm. I am just remembering something my therapist said. She wondered what was going on with him. She wanted me to tell her things about his life, but I didn't know anything, so we dropped it. I have kept him at arm's length pretty much since then and I keep feeling like he wants to be close, but I won't let him. Hmm. And he lost it when I told him I had enlisted in the army. I mean really crazy. I have no idea what that was about for him."

"Perhaps he was scared he was going to lose you. Like really lose you and run out of time to make it right."

"How old are you, Allie? You are like some, I don't know, some wise person."

Allie blushed. "How are you feeling now?"

"Well, shaky. Tired. Empty? Hungry."

"How about you? You said on the phone you had stuff to tell me."

"I did, but I think one big download is enough for one day. Do you mind if I do this another time.? I feel pretty drained from your story."

"Oh, Allie, I didn't mean to dump all of this on you."

Allie took her hand again. "Me being drained by your suffering is not a bad thing. I feel deeply moved. I just, I need to digest how close I feel to you in general. And never closer than today. So, some food?"

"Sure."

CHAPTER 22

Allie hurried across campus to her session with the Dr. Rivera. She seated herself in the client chair. The counselor's room had a standard office desk, but also a seating area in front of floor to ceiling bookshelves sagging from the books stacked on the boards. Her counselor sat in her deep blue upholstered chair and Allie took the matching chair across from her.

"You look breathless today and sort of on the edge of your seat. How did your hike with Lona go yesterday?"

"I need to tell you about some feelings I've been having."

"Okay."

"I think I may be in love with Lona."

Dr. Rivera leaned forward in her chair. "When do you think you started to feel this way?"

"Well, now that I let myself notice more feelings, it was almost immediate. Like from when she helped me after Preston assaulted me. I kept looking at her body and wanting to be around her, and shit, I am going to tell you something that freaked me out." And she proceeded to tell the therapist about the dream of the bear and the sexual feelings she had while being next to Allie in the tent and the feelings she had when

Lona visited the campus.

Her therapist listened quietly and occasionally asked her to elaborate on her experience of herself when she is with Lona and when she is separate. Eventually, she said, "You certainly are describing the kind of feelings and experience that is typical of falling in love. Have you ever felt this way about anyone else? Male or female?"

"Never."

"Hmm. Well, congratulations. This falling in love stuff is one of the better experiences of being human."

"Well. It feels like being totally out of control," Allie replied, her voice tinged with resentment.

"Yes. It does."

"What should I do?"

"Well, we could think of your options."

"I don't want to tell her because she may not feel the same way about me. That would crush me."

"Yep, that is always the fear when we fall in love. There is the possibility that the person we are in love with isn't in love with us."

"Well, how can I know if she is in love with me?"

"Well, you could tell her your feelings and see what she says."

"NO. I want another option."

"Well," the therapist smiled a little. "A lot of people hold in their feelings and see how the other person treats them. They look for evidence that the other person might love them back."

"Okay. Like what evidence?"

"Allie, you have seen a lot of movies about this. I suppose you have read a lot of books where the plot is about falling in love. If you put your good mind into this, you could list the symptoms, or the actions of others that tell us they are in love with us. Why not take that on as an assignment for this week. Oh, and now that you are letting your friends know more of your insides, you could ask them how they know if someone might be in love with them."

"I don't like the word, 'might.' I want to be certain," Allie replied. "You're the doctor. Don't you know the behavior that would be evidence of someone being in love with me?" Allie continued.

"Well, then you can wait until the other person tells you first. Wait for them to take that step first. Most of us try that for a while."

"Okay. That will be my plan. I'll just wait."

"Okay. Good luck with that."

"What do you mean. 'Good luck'. You don't think that plan will work?"

"Not very well when both people are using it."

"I can see why people hate therapy."

"Indeed they do," Dr. Rivera replied.

* * *

I'm feeling lighter, Lona thought as she was driving back to the park. *How weird is that? I slobber and cry like a baby and then I feel lighter. And I like being held by Allie.* She pictured herself being held. Mostly she remembered the physical experience of Allie's arms around her. She remembered the feeling of safety. She remembered sometimes feeling sort of safe when she was surrounded by her comrades in her company. She remembered believing that she would die with or for them and she believed they felt the same way. But being held by Allie was a very different experience. Perhaps this is what Jim meant by landing on an island.

She returned to thinking about her dad. *What if, maybe, dad was dealing with his own guilt? I never thought it was his fault what happened. Well, maybe I did yell at him and blame him initially for putting me in that school. Perhaps I should tell him that.*

CHAPTER 23

Lona was driving the Park truck returning from picking up supplies.

"Hey, Dad. Got time to talk?"

"Lona, yes. I do. What's up"

"I would like to visit next Thursday if that could work for you. I can drive and be there before dinner. I will need to drive home after dinner so I can be at work the next day."

"Sure. No problem. Is anything wrong?"

"I've sort of been working on myself, you know, personal growth stuff. I am trying to figure out some of what made me pull away from you. And I don't want to spend the rest of my life avoiding you."

There was a long silence.

"Dad?" Lona started tapping on the steering wheel, her heart rate elevated.

"I'm here. I am just a mixture of hope and anxiety. Actually, lots of fear. I have hated the superficiality of our relationship. And now I am scared I may somehow blow this and not even have the practiced civility. Whew. Nothing superficial about that report."

"Jeez, Dad. I've never heard you talk that way."

"I know, right? I've been doing some of the personal growth stuff with Ellen. I hate it."

"Me, too. It sucks."

They both laughed. "Is any of this related to your friendship with Allie?"

Lona squirmed in her seat. "I hate being surrounded by people who seem to be more aware of my feelings than I am."

"Right? Ellen is like that. I hate it, and I love it."

"Okay yeah, Allie is sort of turning my world upside down."

"Well, she does have an impressive resume. There is sort of a bidding war here in the Department for her. Please don't tell her that."

"I won't. I guess I would like for you to meet her."

"Oh, honey. I am so happy that you want to bring someone here for me to meet."

"Yeah, I am too. But first things first. Thursday afternoon?"

"Absolutely. See you at the house at 4:00?"

"Great. See you then."

* * *

Lona was still driving back when her phone rang.

"Hi, Chuck. I hope you have some good news."

"Hi, Lona. I had hoped to give you some good news. All of us have been so brain washed by TV crime shows that we expect miracles of evidence gathering. We hope that the forensics will deliver conclusive evidence. There is nothing bad in the forensics, just nothing conclusive. The touch DNA stuff is so easily contaminated and if there is any incidental contact between the victim and the perpetrator, the DNA info is useless. Oh, what I'd give for some blood splatters."

"Okay. Well, shall we separate the crimes and tell me what we've got?" Lona asked.

"Sure. Attempted rape first. The grass clippings were positive for Allie's DNA and Preston's DNA. "

"Good."

"But there was also some of Matt's DNA in the grass clippings. Given what we believe happened, Preston touches and is touched by Matt sexually and so Preston has Matt's touch DNA on his hands and clothes and then he sheds that and his DNA when he attacks Allie. The good news is that none of your DNA was on the grass clippings."

"That's a joke, right?" Lona asked.

"Well, you know your touch DNA was all over Allie's body because of your skin to skin contact in the sleeping bag."

Lona felt the heat rise in her neck and face. "I would not look forward to being on the witness stand against an aggressive attorney."

"Right? Lona, please remember that everything you did that night was to save that young woman and you did save her. It is just that in a court room with a grand-standing attorney, the optics don't seem very good. The picture of two naked women in a sleeping bag would be pretty distracting."

"So we can't definitively state that only Preston and Allie

were at the scene of the rape struggle," Lona stated. There was no blood of Preston on Allie. Only Matt's blood on her shirt. Again, from transfer of Preston's clothes but it just doesn't rule out that Matt might have attacked her at that location or another location."

Lona continued, "Any of Preston's DNA on Allie's wrists or any of his blood mixed with her wounds?"

"No. The rain may have been significant enough to wash much of that away. The touch DNA showed a lot of your contact with her skin."

Lona groaned. "Shit, I was afraid of that. My treating her the way I did for her hypothermia contaminated everything. I suppose my treating her face wounds further contaminated the DNA evidence."

"That and the rain and the drying of her," Chuck replied.

"Shit. Did Preston have any wounds on his right hand that would confirm he hit her?"

"He had some slight bruising of his hand which he claimed he received when he fell on the hike tripping on a root. He said RJ witnessed his fall when they were hiking out. RJ did confirm that."

Lona exhaled a deep breath. "That Preston is turning out to be a wily perpetrator."

"Indeed. Who would have thought he was so intelligent about evidence? His handling of Matt's body seemed pretty inept, but his coverup has been more sophisticated."

"Anything in his interviews, especially before he found out Allie didn't die in the forest that tripped him up?"

"Again, I am sort of embarrassed by how the initial interviews went. They were kind of perfunctory and he got his lawyer involved very early on so that he didn't provide much incriminating information," Chuck said with regret in his voice.

"So it is her word against his and he will say that the facial injuries could have been from Matt, who I suppose is also right-handed.

"Yes," Chuck confirmed.

"Okay. That is the forensics on the attempted rape. And what have we got on Matt's murder?" Lona asked.

"A single blow to the head by an unknown object that left no residue around the wound. So either a metal object or stone. Death was not instantaneous but did occur prior to Matt being placed in the water. There was semen from both Matt and Preston on Matt's clothes. No evidence of anal penetration or bruising. No blood from Preston on any of the material collected from Matt or Preston.

"So, thankfully, Preston's DNA showed up in the semen on Matt's clothes," Lona stated. She continued "So we are left with believing that Preston committed this crime and he then tried to rape Allie and he chased her through the woods, then returned to the camp site and gathered up Matt and Allie's tent and all their belongings and wrapped Matt in all of that and took him into the water and dropped him and then came out and put on dry clothes and crawled back into the tent with RJ and showed surprise when Matt and Allie were gone the next morning. It makes sense if Allie had died in the woods. No witness and even if Matt is found in the water, he can claim

Allie killed him or some unknown assailant had killed them both." Lona continued, "Or we are left to believe that Matt and Allie have a fight and she kills him, and she gathers up the tent and belongings and wraps Matt up and pulls him into the water and then in a crazed episode runs off into the woods wet and in a night shirt. In my mind, the second story seems wildly implausible."

"Same for me," Chuck said. "But the evidence only shows that the location where Allie says she was attacked was the location. The evidence shows she was in a fight with someone."

"How aggressive is your local District Attorney? Would he want to take this case to a jury trial?"

"I think he would prefer to find a settlement. Especially if he is facing a well-known and well-paid defense attorney who will spend a lot of money on expert witnesses who will have the jury feeling like they are back in Chemistry class. It seems like a slam dunk for you and me, but absent Matt's blood on Preston's clothes or shoes, I think there could be reasonable doubt."

"Chuck, how much time did Preston have between leaving the park and being questioned by the police?"

"Approximately five hours."

"Did Preston or RJ say anything about stopping on the way home?"

"Both denied it."

"Your hunch about that?"

"I think they were in a hurry to get home, especially Preston. There were no credit card charges at any of the gas stations and no employees recognized pictures of them having stopped. No camera footage of them entering any of the places along the roads."

"Could you text me the supposed location of the clothing drop-off place and Preston's home address?"

"Lona, what are you planning?"

"I don't know yet. Nothing that would get me in any trouble with harassment or with the prosecution's case. It's just that sometimes if I drive the route and if I recreate Preston's moves, some ideas can come to me."

"That makes sense. Just so you know, our people checked every dumpster along that route, and we thoroughly interviewed people at the clothing drop-off site. And we have canvassed the type of people, mostly homeless, who might have frequented the drop-off site to see if anyone knew anything or has seen anyone wearing the clothes Preston claims to have left in the box."

"Thank you, Chuck. That all sounds very thorough."

"And we obtained a warrant to search Preston's house for any evidence from the hike. We obtained the backpack he used and there was no blood evidence on or in it."

"Hmm. That suggests he either put his clothes in a bag to carry them away, or they never left the woods."

"Did you get a description of the shoes he wore on the camping trip?"

"Yes. We have a good photo of his clothing and shoes from a picture on RJ's phone. Shoes were a fairly common brand of inexpensive trail shoes. We could identify the name and brand from the prints left at the camp. I'll text you the name and a photo of a new pair. He said he left the shoes with the clothes in the box because he wanted nothing to remind him of the tragedy of the weekend."

"Oh, please…"

"Right? A wily character."

"What is Preston's legal status?"

"He is out on bail for the attempted assault on Allie. He is a person of interest in Matt's death."

"Thanks again, Chuck, for keeping me in the loop."

Lona hit the off button on her phone. She thought to herself, *Grandmother, I need a better dream if this case is going to be solved.*

CHAPTER 24

Lona knocked on the door to her dad's condo.

"Hey, Lona, you made good time for DC traffic."

"Yeah, I managed to miss the rush hour grid lock."

"You can put your bag on the chair. Romeo won't get into it."

She knelt down to let the little fur bundle lick her hands and face. "Oh my handsome fella, have you been getting attention on your walks?" The pure white Schnoodle with his large dark eyes followed her into the living room, wagging his tail and hoping for a treat.

"I got nothing for you, you little beggar," she said as she patted the place on the couch for him to jump onto. He plopped his twenty pounds next to her and stretched out.

"I don't know why he likes you so much," her dad said.

"I think I bring lots of smells from the woods with me," Lona replied as she looked around the room. "Have you redecorated? I don't remember this sage color on the walls, or the wood floors. The layout looks the same, but it feels more homey."

"Yes, Ellen has been helping me with the new colors and some of the new furniture and generally just updating and modernizing it. We are thinking of selling our places and getting a larger space together."

"Wow, Dad. I think that is great. Will Ellen be here tonight?"

"Yes, she'll come here after work, probably around 6:00 or so."

Lona let her eyes take in the comfortable room with its gas fireplace and sliding glass doors onto a balcony overlooking the central DC area. "I'll bet the city lights are still gorgeous," she said.

"Yeah, we still get a good view up here on the tenth floor."

Lona got up to look closer at some framed photos on a narrow side table against the wall. She became still as she looked at a framed photo of her mother and father. They were standing on a high ridge overlooking a valley in Canyon de Chelly leading to Spider Rock, a tall obelisk where the Navajo believed the first people emerged from underground to live above the ground. The valley leading to Spider Rock was notably more green than the canyon walls. The view was dramatic and inviting.

'I've never seen this picture before. You both look so young, so handsome and beautiful…"

"And so in love," her father finished for her.

"Why have you never shown me this picture before?"

"I think it was because I found it too painful to look at."

Lona was silent. "And it isn't so painful now?"

Her father cleared his throat. "Well, Ellen has been making me face some of my painful feelings, and she thought you deserved to see this picture. To see the love that made you."

Lona swiped at some tears oozing from her eyes.

"Shit. I guess we are really going to get down to it tonight. We probably could use Ellen here now," Lona murmured.

"That's what I told her. Be here sooner. She told me to pull up my big boy panties and just go for it."

Lona laughed. "I like how she talks to you."

"Me, too. Do you want some coffee, or tea, or beer, or wine?"

"Thanks, Dad. I'll have some tonic water with lime if you have it."

"Coming right up."

He brought her drink and had his version with gin for himself. Lona continued to look at the pictures and found several of her dad and Ellen from various vacation spots.

"I've never seen Ellen in a bathing suit. Was this in the Bahamas?"

"No, it was in St. Bart's: The French islands in the Caribbean."

"I don't mean to be impolite, dad, but Ellen still has quite a figure."

He chuckled. "I will be sure to tell her you said so. She will be thrilled. How is it going with you and Allie?"

"Well, I think I am having feelings that aren't just friendly. I, umm, I like her a lot. But she is from a small town in West Virginia. Lots of, you know, church and stuff. I don't think she knows if she is gay or not. So I am being cautious. I do not want to be her first experience."

"Why is that?"

"Well, I met her in my professional capacity. I sort of saved her life, and I don't want to take advantage of her gratefulness...or something like that."

"Like dating a freshman when you're a senior?" He replied.

"Right. Or dating an employee of yours."

'Right. What is the age difference?"

"Five years."

"Hmm, not too big an age gap," he ventured.

"Yeah, and if I say she acts a lot older than twenty-one, I sound like a pervert trying to justify or minimize the age gap."

"Lona, really, it is just five years. I was five years older than your mother when we met."

"Was she all goo-goo eyed and adoringly dependent?"

"Lona, you, of all people would know your grandmother could never raise an adoringly dependent daughter. Your mom was facing off against me and the Department of the Interior and she did not give an inch in the negotiations. She was driving herself alone all over the reservation doing home health care and being a first responder sometimes to domestic violence. Believe me, she was a force. Like you."

Lona let the silence extend. "You see me that way?"

"Yes, I do. And I love seeing that part of your mom and your grandmother in you. And your beauty always reminds me of your mom."

Again, Lona was silent. Stunned. She felt the heat of pleasure and pain and fear all at the same time. But she had promised herself to ask the hard questions.

"Dad, I talked to Allie about what happened in high school. In the bathroom and after. We have never spoken of that since…"

"I know," he interrupted, "and that is my fault. I felt so guilty. I totally mishandled you coming to live with me. Your grandmother had only one request – protect Lona – and I didn't. I had you in that nest of vipers and I didn't know how to manage my guilt, so I just got angry." He looked down at his hands, not meeting her eyes.

Lona felt stunned and awkward. Then she reached out and put her hands on his. "Wow. We both felt guilty. I believed I had let you and all my relatives down by acting like a wild Indian. I scared myself, dad, with my rage. I was so scared and ashamed."

He looked up. And now Lona could not meet his eyes. He moved closer to her and put his arm around her shoulder.

"I was never ashamed of you. I was ashamed of myself."

Lona felt some wall in herself crumble. "Oh, Dad. I am so sorry I shut off from myself and from you."

"That goes both ways, Lona." He took a tissue for himself and handed one to her. He cleared his throat. "Well, at least Ellen will be proud of me."

Lona chuckled. "Allie will be proud of me, too. She told me she thought perhaps you felt guilty. I had never put that together."

"How could you? You were just a kid. I was the one who abandoned you during that time."

"Well, yeah. You kind of did. But you were, you know, trying to make it up to me once I got into the public high school. We did okay then. But when I joined the Army, you went ballistic."

"God, this is hard," he sighed. "To revisit my worst parenting moments. But here goes. I didn't understand why you would throw all your potential away to enlist in the army. My God, I was scared again, even more scared that I couldn't protect you."

"But Dad, I needed to find a place where I belonged. And the army gave me that. I could be all my tomboy self and get promoted for all my fierceness and I could control my rage. I got more comfortable with my power and my sexuality."

"I know. I saw the difference in you when you came back. Especially once you had gotten through all the rehab."

"And Dad, thanks for visiting me so much during that time. I felt then that you were in my corner. But by then my habit of distance was just too practiced with you."

"You know, Lona, I started therapy as soon as I saw you in the hospital. I couldn't handle all my feelings then."

"I didn't know that."

"Well, yeah. My therapist wasn't as good as Ellen. But he did help me get back to functioning. We worked on my grief over your mother's death. Which I had never really processed."

"Oh, that must have been very hard."

'It was."

"Dad?"

"Yes."

"That's enough for me for tonight. Can we spend some time being superficial or just, you know, talking about my next career move?" Lona asked.

"As long as it doesn't involve tight-rope walking in a circus without a net," he replied.

"Deal."

Ellen let herself in the door and saw them on the couch surrounded by snotty tissues. She smiled and walked past them into the kitchen carrying her bags of food. "I picked up some great Chinese take-out for dinner. You guys hungry?"

"Famished," they said in unison.

* * *

Lona felt exhausted on her drive back to the park. *I can't believe what I told Dad. I can't believe what he told me. I can't believe how right Allie was. I can't believe who my dad has become since he has been with Ellen; who he has become with Ellen. Having the right partner is so important. They remind me of Jim and Mary. I have missed so much being distant from him. I am not going to keep avoiding him. And I am not going to avoid Ellen.* She pictured the photo of her mom and dad again. *I should pay attention to this feeling I am having now. It is like a tingling in my chest and a soft hum in my lower back. That is strange ... Hell, just feeling my own body seems strange. Well, and here comes me remembering Allie being asleep on my shoulder. Oops, here comes that feeling much lower. Shit. Stop it.*" But her body wouldn't let her stop it.

* * *

"Hey, Lona, how did the visit go?" Allie asked.

"It was surreal. My dad was a version of himself I didn't recognize."

"A good version?"

"A fabulous, warm, loving, crying, strong version."

"And you? Did you share with him about the bathroom episode?"

"Yes. That and lots of other stuff. I sort of didn't recognize me," Lona replied.

"Fabulous, warm, loving, crying, and strong?" Allie responded.

"I don't recognize the strong. But I was full-on vulnerable. We went through a lot of tissues."

"Oh, Lona, I am so proud of you."

"Weirdly, I am proud of myself. And proud of my dad. He showed me a picture of my mom and him when they were together. He has never had any pictures of her in his condo."

"Perhaps it was too painful?" Allie ventured.

"Allie, sometimes you freak me out. That was what he said. He said that Ellen has been helping him deal with some of his pain and she thought it would be good for me to see some photos of them together."

"Wow. She sounds like a keeper. Encouraging him to have

a photo of another woman displayed."

"Ellen and Dad want to meet you."

"I would look forward to that. On another note, how are you doing with the idea of coming to my graduation?"

"Yes, I will do some trades at work so I can get some time off on that weekend. How is your therapy going?"

"Hmm. I am embarrassed to say I should have gone to therapy earlier in my life. It seems I have some unresolved stuff around Frankie's death."

"Well, you and I both get to hang out in some regret this evening."

"Yes, regret and happiness."

"Allie, you are having some moments of happiness?" Lona asked.

Allie thought to herself, *yeah whenever I have contact with you.*

"Hmm. Yes, some moments of happiness are creeping in. I think it is mostly some hope about the future."

"Yeah, I can tell from what dad has said that he thinks you will be a great hire."

"That reminds me," Allie interrupted. "I got a letter from the Department, and they want me to show up for orientation four days after my graduation. So I will be busy moving and finding a place to live."

"Oh, Allie, that is great," Lona exclaimed. "I can help you with that. I can rent a truck and help move you once you have secured a place. I am sure you will have a great career ahead of you in DC."

Allie got quiet. She noticed that Lona only talked about HER future. Not OUR future.

"Well, I gotta go. Thanks for calling. I have a paper I still have to finish," Allie said brusquely.

"Okay. Yeah, get back to work." Lona hung up. *That was kind of abrupt. I wonder if I said something wrong? Did I somehow put pressure on Allie?* She felt her mood shift and some anxiousness creeped in.

CHAPTER 25

Allie seated herself in the client chair. She pulled out her tablet with the list of signs that someone likes you romantically.

"I see you have done your homework," Dr. Rivera noted.

"Yes, and it is confusing because sometimes the very same behaviors mean opposite things."

"Okay. Hmm. Tell me more," Dr. Rivera said, sitting more deeply into her chair.

"Well, I've polled all my girlfriends and there are the usual signs like the person spends time with you, they guard the time, they don't cancel last minute. They touch you, not just sexually. They stare at your lips and maybe other places on your body. They ask about you and seem to remember what you have told them. They laugh and joke with you. Ooh, and they plan meetings or events with you out into the future: Not just one week, but like, a month or so. Like they hope to still be seeing you in the future. Oh, and they introduce you to their friends AND to their family. That one seemed big for everyone. They want to take you to special events. They spend money on you (that one seems a little outdated). But special efforts on your birthday. Valentine's Day is a critical test."

"All that seems spot on," her therapist replied and shifted in her seat to sip some hot tea.

"Right? But then if they have some kind of mixed feelings…like being afraid of commitment, or not sure of you, then they might do some opposite stuff."

"Opposite stuff?"

"Like little or inconsistent contact or even being critical or sarcastic. Like if they are afraid of their feelings, they might push you away."

"Okay, I got it," Dr. Rivera replied. "Like the boy who pulls your pigtails because he likes you. Oops, sexist. Like the girls who … I don't have any grade school examples for girls. Do you?"

"No. I didn't even know girls had sexual feelings. Well, Mom would say some girls are 'boy crazy.' I took that to be a bad thing."

"And you were never 'boy crazy'?"

"No. But also never girl crazy. Not until now."

"Have you ever asked Lona about her past relationships? Do you have any evidence she is gay?"

"No. We've been kind of busy dealing with all the death and dying stuff, and the impending trial stuff. And we've been getting to know each other. She asked me to be her friend. I don't feel comfortable asking her about her past relationships. She knows I am a virgin."

"How did she find that out?" Dr. Rivera asked, raising her eyebrows.

"I told her. I was very vulnerable about Matt and somehow, I blurted out that she probably thought I was pathetic."

"What did she say to that?"

"She said I might be innocent but that I was also blah, blah, blah."

"What was the blah?

"Oh, you know, stuff like I am smart and brave and funny," Allie said with a dismissive wave of her hand.

"Have you heard that about yourself before?"

"Sometimes. But what I want to know is if she obsesses about me. If she wants to have sex with me. If she has sexual dreams about me. If she might want to be in a committed relationship with me."

"Sounds like you want to know if she is as crazy about you as you are about her."

"Exactly ... How can I find that out? And don't tell me I have to ask her!" Allie said vehemently, crossing her arms across her chest.

"Okay." Dr. Rivera was quiet.

"You think that may be my only way, don't you?" Allie continued.

"That is certainly a clear way. Sometimes another way is to create situations of close physical contact and see if she will take the first step in a truly clear way."

Allie leaned forward in her chair. "Tell me more."

"Well," Dr Rivera took another sip of her tea. "See if she will be the one to start a kiss. Or a hug that really lingers and becomes, you know, like really pressing your bodies together."

Allie was silent. She reviewed their experiences of holding each other while in emotional pain. None of that had turned sexual, well, except the thing that happened in the tent.

"What are you thinking about now, Allie?" Dr. Rivera softy asked.

"Well, Lona has started telling me some of her past family stuff. She's had some deaths in her family and some trauma with a gang of mean girls. She has cried with me. She has let me hold her. And of course, I have slobbered all over her."

"So she cries and you slobber?"

"What is your point?" Allie asked irritably, shifting in her chair, and crossing her arms again.

"Really, Allie? You don't see or hear how you are so critical of your feelings, but not hers? Her pain, but not yours?"

Allie was silent.

"Well, when you say it that way, it sounds like maybe I need to be nicer or more compassionate towards myself." Allie ventured.

"Ya think?"

"Well, lately I am learning that when people cry with each other, it means they feel safe with each other. And my friends do that with me now. But I still don't know if Lona just feels safe with me. I don't know if she just feels protective of me. Do you think she might be gay or have sexual feelings towards me?" Allie asked.

"For that you have to spend some money on a psychic and hope you get a good one," Dr. Rivera sat back with a smile.

"What if I have fallen in love with her and she isn't in love with me?" Allie said softly.

"Then you will be very disappointed. And hurt. But letting

ourselves have romantic feelings always comes with risk. You have been on the bench for some time now. It does take courage to get off the bench and get in the game."

Allie sighed deeply. "Yeah. Well, this is such a new game for me. I don't like being so insecure."

"You could always just run away, use avoidance to manage your anxiety."

"Did you learn that in school? Just to be provocative?" Allie responded.

"Of course. Is it working?"

"Sort of. I don't want to stay so avoidant and numb."

"Well, there you have it. Just stay with the process. Trust that you are strong enough to handle whatever comes your way."

Silence.

Dr. Rivera leaned forward and looked deeply into Allie's eyes. "Allie, the young woman sitting here with me is strong enough to survive this disappointment, if that is what happens."

"I hope so," Allie said softly.

* * *

"How is the research going on people indebted to Preston's dad and anyone with a history of sexual crimes?" Lona asked Chuck.

"Ahh, everyone in town is indebted to the construction company in one way or another. And no one has showed up on social media with a newly acquired brassiere. What I did find when I looked at employees and at Mr. Stuart's real estate holdings was that RJ has an older brother and father who work for Mr. Stuart. And Mr. Stuart owns both their houses. And of course, RJ is an adolescent who might participate in a pantie raid if he were in college."

"I think we should set a trap," Lona replied. And she proceeded to share her plan with Chuck.

* * *

Lona decided to drive to Preston's house. And then to the location where he claimed that he left his clothes and shoes. But first, she pulled over at the state operated Liquor store to obtain a bottle of wine for the next time she had a dinner at Jim and Mary's house.

She left the store hoping that the employee had steered her correctly with one bottle that would go well with chicken and one to accompany beef.

"Hey, cutie." The voice came from a group of young men gathered around several vehicles parked in the shade of a large oak tree at the edge of the parking lot. Lona estimated them to be in their early to mid-twenties. The boys were sitting on truck running boards or slouched against the doors, passing around a bottle of brown liquid that could only be sold at the store she was exiting. Lona approached her Jeep. *Perhaps I should have worn my uniform,* she thought. She kept her head down and didn't make any eye contact.

"Come on, Sweetie, you can at least give us a look." One of the young men stepped away on an angle to intercept her. "I'll give you a shot of this good stuff for a smile."

Lona altered her course hoping to avoid him. He continued his advance, and she slowed her pace and raised her head looking directly into his eyes.

"No, thank you," she said in a neutral tone. She noticed the other men shift closer to their leader as she looked at the followers more closely. She was trying to judge their mood and level of intoxication. She saw one of the followers hanging back. "RJ, is that you?" she called out to him. He lowered his head and remained silent.

'Hey, sweetie, look at me. I'm the one with the bottle. And how do you know RJ?" he asked. She remained silent. "Hey, aren't you that Indian who got our friend, Preston in trouble?"

Lona ignored him and resumed her walk.

"RJ, how does this woman who is clearly not from around here know you?" He reached out and grabbed Lona's arm that was carrying her bag of wine bottles. Lona quickly pivoted, stepping back towards him, and slamming her foot down on his instep and then moving away, placing her bag on the ground. She had used her free arm to grab his bottle out of his hand and then moved out of his reach.

"What the fuck," he yelled as he swayed to get his feet under him.

"Let's not waste this bottle," she said. "I will place it carefully on the ground and go on my way if that works for you." She looked him squarely in his unfocused eyes and placed the bottle out of his reach on the ground. Then she picked up her bag and got into her Jeep. As she drove near RJ, she rolled down her window. "RJ, you need to pick better friends."

"Whatever," he said turning away from her.

I am so glad I didn't grow up here, she thought as she proceeded to drive to the downtown area.

As she drove through what seemed to be the main street, she noticed the architecture of a few of the older buildings. The brick and mortar had the expensive details that were common in the early to mid-1900s. Those buildings needed repair and seemed empty. And several of the newer store fronts were closed.

This place was once a hub for the surrounding area. It was a functioning small town. And now it's like the railroad went to another place and it has withered. Somehow the economy no longer supports this town.

She remembered what Allie had said about the loss of jobs. She continued to let her maps program direct her through some of the older residential areas where mature trees softened the sense of poverty but could not hide it. *This reminds me of how I feel when I'm on the Rez.* On the outskirts of the town near the highway were some fast-food places and the stores that specialized in inexpensive merchandise. She took a side road off the highway and drove slowly in front of the address that was where Preston's family lived. There was a sign at the edge of the property that read Stuart and Sons, Construction Company.

She wondered if the family had any daughters, and what the sign meant to them. The residence was partially obscured by the trees. It was sitting higher up on the sloping hill. The construction offices were in a one-story building that seemed typical of small businesses. There were other buildings scattered on the property. It seemed they housed various types of construction equipment and trucks.

I wonder what kind of pressure Preston would experience if he weren't a 'real man.' I need to ask Chuck about the number of sons and Preston's birth order. I wonder how many sons this business can sustain. There could be a lot of good hiding places on this property. But also, a lot of eyes if it were the middle of the day and all the employees were coming and going.

She sat quietly, imagining a desperate and sleep deprived Preston. She couldn't picture him sneaking out of the house in daylight to bury or burn his clothes. She entered the address of the clothing drop off place on her maps program. It took her twenty minutes to drive back to town. On the edge of the downtown area, behind the main and side streets of the mostly abandoned buildings was a rundown building that had a Salvation Army sign. Here the services for the indigent seemed as inadequate as the services for the working poor.

She got out of her car and approached a sign that said donations. She saw some bags of donated and used clothes. This area was behind the entrance to the building. It was reached by driving by in an alley. There were some stationary plastic boxes and a tarp over the area to keep the rain off the donated items. She went around to the front of the building and entered the front door.

"Can I help you?" asked the middle- aged woman sitting at a desk littered with paperwork. Lona noted her pleasant tone.

"I hope so. My name is Lona Johnson. I am gathering some background information to assist in the investigation of Matt Carlson's death."

"Oh, you must be that park ranger that helped Allie. We are all grateful for what you did."

"Hmm. I am a little surprised you know of me."

"Well, it is a small town and I go to the same church as Allie and Matt's moms. I have watched both of those young people grow up. Both of them were members of our church. Allie helps out with the choir and sometimes with the Sunday school." She started to tear up. And then took a deeper breath. "How can I help you?"

Lona looked at her name tag. "Well, Martha White, I am seeking some background information. You aren't related to the flour company are you?"

"I am afraid not. But I do use their flour."

Lona smiled and sat down in the chair adjacent to the desk. "I drove by the home and business of the Stuart family, and I am seeking some information on them and Preston. For example, do you know how many kids are in the family?"

"Sure. Preston is the youngest of three boys. And there is one girl. The two older boys are employed in the business."

"And does the daughter work for the business?"

Martha smiled. "You saw the sign, Stuart and Sons?"

"Yes. I did"

"Well Mr. Stuart is a pulled himself up by his bootstraps kind of guy and he is, like many men his age, a little old-fashioned."

"And the daughter?"

"She got married after her freshman year at college. She found herself a nice young man and started a family. They moved to Kentucky."

"How would you describe Mr. Stuart?"

"He runs a successful business. He is very hard-working."

"Is he well liked in the town?"

Martha paused. "I think he is well-respected. And he provides some jobs and that is a lifesaver in this town. He has been successful in building vacation homes for people from Virginia and Kentucky. And even some people from the north. He is meticulous and demanding, but I think he is fair to his employees."

"And to his family?"

Again, Martha paused.

"Martha, are you following that saying, 'if you can't say something nice about someone, don't say anything at all?' I am asking because sometimes in order to solve a crime, I need to know the emotional life of the people involved."

Martha took a deep breath, considering her words. "Okay. Preston's dad is very controlling in his family. His wife and children keep the peace by being obedient. His wife also helps the economy by spending his money."

"Does she volunteer here?"

"Heavens, no. She practices a different religion."

Lona raised her eyebrows. "So, is she Jewish?" Lona asked.

"Oh, no. Nothing like that. Just, you know, not the widows and orphans and…"

"Not based on the compassion of Jesus?" Allie finished Martha's sentence.

"Exactly," Martha confirmed.

"Was Preston obedient to his father?"

"Preston seems to be a disappointment to his dad. He took after his uncle, his dad's brother. More a life of drinking and hunting, and then the military."

"Yeah, he wore his uncle's military clothes."

"The ones the police are looking for?"

"Right."

"We searched this place high and low but the donation area is in the back behind our building and people come and go and we never see them. We put that in the back for a reason."

"To lessen people's shame if they need something?" Lona guessed.

"Exactly."

'Martha, you and your women are indeed doing God's work here."

"I hope so. Sometimes it can be so discouraging."

"Right. I think so too. Can we return to the relationship Preston had with his father?"

"Sure. Hmm. Preston was the better athlete of the boys. But his dad was pretty hard on him. Preston wanted to get a scholarship in football and he did one year at a small college on a partial scholarship. Then he got injured, his knee or something, and he came home. He has been drinking and he does some of the manual parts of the business. But he seems like an angry, lost young man."

"You said his dad could be hard on him?"

"His dad had a reputation of being obnoxious at the football games. He would yell at the officials and at Preston if he made any obvious mistakes. So, yeah. I think his dad could be hard on all his boys."

"Any history of violence that you know of with Preston?"

"Not that I know of. Perhaps some alcohol and car problems. But if so, his dad would have fixed that."

"Do you think Preston has gotten involved with any of the drug business?'

"Not that I know of. I think most of the lost kids find their way to marijuana. We have a lot of angry lost young men. There are so few jobs for them. The ones with ambition tend to move away where they can find work."

Lona paused. "The parent's marriage?"

"There have been some rumors that both of them may struggle with fidelity."

Lona smiled and handed Martha a staff card and wrote her cell phone number on it. "Please take this and if you hear anything more or think of anything that might shed any light on this situation, please do not hesitate to call me. What you have told me today is very helpful."

Martha got up from behind her desk and came around and

gave Lona a hug. "You be careful, Lona. Angry lost men can be dangerous."

"Thank you, Martha, for all you are doing to try to save people, one at a time."

Lona walked out of the office, feeling like her soul had received a refreshing snack from meeting a Martha. *This town seems to have its share of good, hard working people and then its share of people who are struggling, and then those that are just no good. I guess it is like any place.*

* * *

Lona's Dream

I am sleeping in a camp site. I am curled up in a blanket. I wake up and it is cold, and I hear a noise in the woods. I get out of my blanket and follow the noise. Someone or some animal is moving through the woods. I hear twigs break, footsteps shuffle, branches swing with the passage of something large moving through them.

I see a faint animal trail and I follow it. The noise is in front of me. Whatever I hear is also on this trail. My foot hits a root and I fall. I am next to a moss-covered large tree trunk. It fell to the forest floor a long time ago. I am not hurt. The noise in front of me has stopped. I wake up.

Allie's Dream

I am nestled into a small cave that has been dug into a hillside. I am cold and there is a presence in the small cave. Some arm or paw pulls me away from the side of the cave. The arm pulls me into a furry, warm blanket. I feel safe and comforted. The furry blanket shifts. I am being held by a woman. She is touching my breasts and I am shifting to touch her breasts. My mouth is on her nipple and I hear her groaning and I am getting so aroused.

I awake and my hand is on my clitoris and I keep touching myself until I climax. I am fully awake now. I am not in a cave. I am in my bed at school and I am totally freaked out.

* * *

Lona kept thinking, *What can I get Allie for her graduation? A watch? A necklace? I wonder what her spirit animal might be? That makes no sense. She is not an Indigenous Person. A blouse? Her own pool cue? What she really needs is an end to her anxiety about the court stuff. Now that the forensic report is complete and ambiguous except for sex between Preston and Matt, I think it is only a few days before Preston's lawyer pushes for a plea bargain and succeeds in getting a minimal sentence for assault on Allie.*

She called Chuck, "Hey there. I think we should spring the trap tonight. Can you be available for watching my cottage?"

"Sure. I will swing by the office and happily announce that you found the blood-soaked clothes and will bring them in tomorrow. And that you will be in some mandatory training tonight in Morgantown that lasts until 8:30pm. And that the clothes are secure in your cottage, and you will bring them in tomorrow. And Jim will also be available?"

"I will call him next. I will leave my car in his closed garage and be sure to not turn on any lights." We'll see what we can catch. Hopefully, the threat of bringing in the clothes tomorrow will get them worried enough to do something tonight. I assume they will wait till it is just after dark."

CHAPTER 26

Lona sat quietly in the chair in a corner of her room. She had stuffed pillows on her bed to look like someone was sleeping. She was too anxious to sleep. Sometime around 9:30 she heard a noise coming from behind the cottage. She slipped out of the chair and crawled quietly in that direction. There were no doors or windows on that side of the cottage. She heard what sounded like water sloshing and footfalls. Then she smelled gasoline. She quickly went to the unlocked window on the side of the cottage. She lowered herself outside and started running towards the dark form that was surrounded by three empty gas cans. She saw him raise his arm and was holding a lighter towards the wall. She yelled for him to drop it and he turned towards her just as she ran into him hitting his arm sideways and knocking the lighter out of his hand and away from the cottage wall. They tumbled to the ground, and she was yelling for help as he rolled her over onto her back. She managed to get two hands on his arm that was cocked to hit her and she swung him sideways with all her might just when Chuck and Jim joined the fight and had him turned on his stomach and got his hands behind his back to cuff him. Once cuffed Jim turned his flashlight on the face of the intruder.

"Well, I guess we know now who was responsible for the prior break-in, Mr. Stuart. But the gasoline takes this to a whole new level."

"I don't know what you're talking about. You have no right to man handle me."

"You have the right to remain silent…" Chuck began.

* * *

CHAPTER 27

"Well, Lona, it seems our trap worked on getting the vandal caught." Chuck said. "I will call our forensic people and get all the evidence collected. He will probably bond out tomorrow, but these will be hefty charges. You don't need to stay here if you want to go to sleep."

"We have a spare bedroom, if you want, Lona. There will be a lot of noise here for a few more hours.," Jim added.

"I would love that, but there is something I must do. I've been putting it off. I need to return to the crime scene. I need to spend the night out there."

"You think you missed some evidence you can find at night?"

"I know it sounds crazy. It feels crazy. But I keep getting the same dream over and over and it starts at the crime scene. You know my people think that spirits communicate with us through dreams. And okay, I know how crazy that sounds to you."

"Lona, I have lived long enough to have a pretty big 'perhaps column,'" Jim responded.

"What?"

"The 'perhaps column.' The unknown, the magical.

The Quantum Entanglement."

"What?"

"Some scientists keep finding suggestions that plants communicate with each other. And some scientists are looking at how subatomic particles can have an influence on each other over a vast distance. We don't know the mechanisms for this. Oh, and twins and people close to each other know when someone dies before they are told. Well, you get it. Magic. Or the unknown or Hope.

"Do you guys have any books on this?"

"I'll ask Mary to find it."

"Great. And can we do dinner next week?" I need to get to Allie's graduation tomorrow night."

"You got it."

Chuck chimed in. "Well, since we really don't have the blood soaked clothes, I am certainly hoping you find them so I don't have to back track with people in my office about the misinformation I fed them."

* * *

Lona arrived at the empty camp site after midnight. The night was clear, and the stars were flung across the sky like diamonds on black velvet. She had brought the minimal camping gear. She had packed baggies for any crime scene evidence and gloves to insure she would not leave any of her DNA on anything she found. She had worked out a general time frame of when Preston had started each activity and when he might have completed each part of the crimes and the cover up. She decided to take a brief nap so that she could be more alert, and she set her watch alarm for an hour and laid down on the padded ground cover she had brought.

She felt her eyes get heavy as she stared at the stars and they got even more heavy as she pictured her grandmother being with her. She remembered the smell of her grandmother: wood smoke, lavender, and pinyon.

Lona's Dream

I wake up under the stars and they are bright. I can see Ursa Major so clearly and as I watch, there is a shooting star near the handle of the big dipper. I hear a huffing noise and I turn my head and locate the noise over by the lake. I see an animal pelt on the ground by the water. I don't recognize the animal that once wore the fur. The huffing noise is near the pelt. Then the noise moves towards the woods and I follow it. The faint animal trail seems like the one I've had in other dreams. I catch a glimpse of dark fur. Again, I think it is a bear. I call out my grandmother's first clan name, but the bear ignores me. It now has the pelt in its mouth. I see a large fallen tree covered with moss. The bear stops and looks at me. I start to follow it, but it growls and turns and moves on. I don't follow. I wake up and it is three minutes till my alarm will go off.

That was a doozy of a dream. Clearly I need to follow an animal trail. But why start at the lake? And what does the pelt mean? Let's see, Preston attacks Allie, she runs into the woods headed towards my camp, he follows. He has on his clothes then. He returns. He packs up all the belongings of Matt and Allie and stuffs everything in their packs. He wraps all of this around Matt. He takes Matt to the lake. He is quiet. He doesn't want to wake RJ. Does he take off his clothes before he drags Matt into the lake? Does he take his clothes off afterwards? He has to be cold and shivering. Does he get dry clothes from his tent before he disposes of his blood-stained clothes? Well, let's get started.

She traces Preston's movements giving each its allotted time, starting at the kill site of Matt. Then she moves to the assault on Allie, picturing in detail the events that while brief are uncomfortable to picture. She then runs into the woods chasing Allie in a chaotic manner. It was hard to re-create the wandering after Allie. She doesn't know if Preston had a flashlight. She imagines that he gets more frantic as the time passes. She imagines that he convinces himself that she could not possibly survive in her thin T-shirt. After about thirty minutes, she heads back in the general direction of Preston's camp site, wondering if he got lost on the way back. She goes to the spot of Allie's tent and imagines Preston hurrying to roll up the tent and putting all the gear into the two backpacks. Then lugging both to where Matt's body is. He has to touch the body. He has to wrap the dead weight of the packs around the dead weight of Matt. Did he take everything in trips to the lake and then wrap Matt or wrap him where he lay and then carry all of that weight to the lake. She decides he had to do it in trips. Now to get Matt out deep enough into the water. She decides to take her own clothes off and imagine trying to float Matt out. Was there enough air in the bags to lessen the weight? She imagines letting the weight of Matt slip under the water. And the relief of getting back to the land. She puts on her own dry clothes and imagines that Preston had dry clothes of his own.

Now what? Does the pelt represent Matt's blood-stained clothes? In the dream the bear moved off in the direction towards the Park entrance. Perhaps Preston didn't want to go in the direction that Allie had fled. She stands still and waits to feel the direction of the faint wind coming off the lake. It is blowing away from the path that Allie took into the woods.

Most established camp sites have several trails leading away from the tent area into the woods. Campers take these trails as they use the woods for their bathroom. Lona decides to follow the most used trail with the wind at her back. It isn't very far before the trail ends and then she just bushwhacks continuing in the general direction she had started. She takes the way that has the least dead fall and the fewest vines. She finds herself looking for fallen trees but could see very little due to the dim light.

I wonder again if Preston had a flashlight. He had to have been tired. Would he dare use the flashlight if he was afraid of being caught? She wandered for about thirty minutes. I can't imagine him spending any more time than this. And I can't see anything. I think I'll rest by this tree and nap and wait until dawn and then look some more.

* * *

Lona opened her eyes as she heard the birds begin their dawn chatter. She felt rested. She decided to sing as much of the various chants that she could remember. *If the spirits are around they will think I am pathetic. They will ask themselves why this lazy girl didn't learn better. I will call out our clan names. I am on more solid ground there.* She went through the clan names several times so the spirits could find her. She felt calmer and paused. Now she was hearing lots of squirrel noise as they chased each other up and down the trees.

Okay, you guys over there. You are being particularly intrusive. You are making it hard for me to be calm. Don't make me drag out my sling shot. She smiled. *What I wouldn't give for some good pancakes right now.* She slowly got up and stretched. She moved carefully toward the racket of the squirrels and saw they were chasing each other all over a fallen tree with lots of moss. She watched them with delight, rooting for the smaller of the two. They scurried to the far side of the tree, and then one of them appeared to have some fabric in his mouth. Lona stopped breathing. She was afraid to hope and yet, she did. She went around the trunk and saw that the squirrels had piled up the earth around something they had partially dug up. It was a nylon bag.

She fell to her knees and started the chant of thankfulness. She called out the clan names and the Navajo word for squirrels. She got to her feet and danced for joy. She called out to her grandmother and thanked her for working so hard to give her the clues. Wiping the tears from her eyes, she put on her crime scene gloves and took pictures of the hole and the bag and the surrounding area. Then she put the nylon bag into the evidence bag, peeking through the hole made by the squirrel. She confirmed that the cloth inside was the camouflage pattern.

As Lona walked back towards the park entrance, she imagined the relief she could provide to Allie. This is the best graduation present ever, she thought.

* * *

"Hey Chuck, can you meet me at the Ranger Station?'

"Sure. The whole office is buzzing about our arrest of Mr. Stuart last night. And his lawyer did get him bonded out this morning. But the evidence is solid."

"Have you told them yet that we made up the rumor of the clothes being found?"

"Not yet."

"Well, now you can tell them the news that the clothes really have been found," Lona continued. "I really did find Preston's blood-soaked clothes!! I need you to get them to the detectives and stop any plan for plea bargaining for Preston. This changes everything."

"Oh, Lona. This is the Christmas present in May. Did you actually find them last night when you went to the woods? That is insane. It was dark. How on Earth did you find them?"

"Hard work and luck."

"Where did you find them?"

"About one hundred yards from the crime scene camp site. They were buried under a fallen tree. How long before you can get here?"

"I will call immediately. I think it will take a couple of hours to round up the right people. This is just coming in under the wire. The meeting with Preston was scheduled for tomorrow. You know you can't tell Allie yet. We don't want Preston skipping town."

"I know. Mum's the word."

"Whew!! Unbelievable. And I want more details. See you soon."

CHAPTER 28

Good smells met her at the door.

"Hail the conquering hero," Jim said with a big smile. "I can't wait to hear all the story."

"Luckily, I brought a good bottle of wine," Lona said, holding it in one hand while Jim enveloped her in a hug.

"I'm sorry I left you with all the work at the park. Those detective guys had me occupied the whole day. I had to take them to the location of the scene. And they had to take all their own photos and measure distance, etc."

"I gathered you found the missing clothes. And that will prove Allie's innocence once and for all and convict Preston."

"Yep. I did find the blood-soaked clothes." She proceeded to give Jim and Mary the details as they ate the delicious pot roast and home-made bread. She included a report of her dreams and the squirrels.

"You must be exhausted. Did you get any sleep?" Mary asked.

"Yeah, I found the clothes shortly after dawn and I took a nap before the forensic guys got there.

"Have they arrested Preston yet?" Jim asked.

"I don't know how quickly they will act. I hope they pick

him up before they analyze the blood samples, though that should be faster than the other forensic work. They only have to confirm Matt's blood on the clothes. But if he was going to run, he probably heard the news yesterday when we used that to flush out the vandal. Once the forensics are done, I think they will bring new charges and there will be a plea bargain and no trial."

"How much time do you think he will get?"

"Hard for me to say. If his attorney gets it to manslaughter and obstruction of justice and attempted rape, it will be a substantial amount of time. At least Allie doesn't have to face the experience of a trial. And she will feel safer with Preston in prison."

"You handed them all the evidence they need on a silver platter."

"I didn't give them any of the dream information or my chanting. I told them it was just perseverance and good luck. I chalked up the squirrel part to good luck."

"Yep. Good old fashioned good luck," Mary said, laughing. "Speaking of perseverance, I heard you and your father are on a new footing with each other."

"I'll say. We both had some guilt and shame about some stuff from the past. We got it dissected, and I think, healed. You know, we talked, we cried, we hugged."

They all laughed again.

"Seriously, I don't know when I have felt so grateful and so happy," Lona said.

"Oh, Lona, that is so good to hear. Now, if I'm prying,

please tell me to mind my own business."

"Now, Mary," Jim interrupted.

"Don't 'now Mary' me, Jim. I can ask."

"Oops, okay," Jim backed off.

"Lona, I have gotten the impression that maybe you are developing a special friendship with Allie."

"Oh Mary. That language is so southern and quaint. Yes. I have discovered an uncomfortable amount of special feelings for Allie," Lona admitted with a smile.

"Uncomfortable?" Mary asked.

Jim squirmed and Mary ignored him. Lona smiled.

"Mary, I have come to, um, to be, um, very attracted to Allie. Like in a romantic way."

"Ah, honey, that is fabulous. No wonder you want to read books on relationships."

Jim intervened. "Mary, we can just let Lona, you know, take her time to tell us what she wants to tell us, when she wants to tell us."

Both Mary and Lona looked at Jim as he squirmed some more. Their eyes met and both smiled.

"I got this, Mary," Lona said."Jim, I like how you have respected me and our professional relationship. And I am comfortable expanding that to a friendship, especially since I have decided to leave the National Park Service."

"What?"

"I love the woods and they have been such a big part of my recreation and healing. But I do not see my future being in the Park Service. I don't think I have the patience for it and if I stay, it might rob me of the pleasure I take in the woods."

"Do you know what you want to do for work?"

"I think I do. The part I really like about work is helping others. I don't want to do that in a rule setting and enforcing way. I want to actually go to college and learn how to help people, um, perhaps as a counselor. I got so much help from the book Mary loaned me and I got excited about psychological stuff."

"Is this something you and your father talked about?" Mary asked.

"Yeah. We did. After all the crying stuff. I know it will be a long process, but I have some GI benefits I can use. My mother invested the money my dad sent her, and it has been growing over time. And it turns out, my dad has put some money aside for me. He has always been supportive of me getting more education. It has taken me awhile to get over my 'I'm so stupid' voice in my head. When I am learning things that hold my attention, I get pretty good grades. And this personal growth stuff really holds my attention. And I think I have enough patience now to make myself learn other things that aren't as stimulating but are necessary."

Mary got up from the table and came around and hugged her.

"Oh, Honey. That sounds great. I know you can do this."

Lona cleared her throat. "Thanks, Mary. That means a lot to me."

"And Allie? How will that work with your plans with her?"

"Well, she will start working in DC after she graduates, and

I will apply to a junior college there to get my required classes and then transfer to a four-year college for the classes in my major. So we should be in the same town."

"Have you told her any of this?"

"No. I've been trying to keep the relationship on a professional, well, actually, a friendship basis. I needed to wait until all this trial stuff was resolved."

"Do you think she feels the same way about you? Like in a romantic way?"

Lona paused. "Jeez, I really hope so. We talk every day on the phone. I sort of got the feeling that I am the one holding back. But maybe. Oh, shit. I don't know." A look of worry came over Lona's face. "I am pretty sure she is gay. I think she may be realizing that for herself. She is seeing a counselor for all the assault stuff. Her graduation is tomorrow night, and I will be driving there for that. I want to tell her the news about no trial in person. I think this news will be a better present than a nice pen. Thank you guys for the dinner. Can I help with the dishes?"

"Right. Just put your girlfriend on hold while you do the dishes. Get outta here," both of them insisted.

* * *

"Hey, Allie. Good to hear your voice."

"Lona, Hi."

"Are you ready for graduation day?"

"I am both excited and scared. I got the employment offer and I've been researching apartments in DC. So far, I am checking the time limits at the Youth Hostel. You know, how long can someone stay there? I never dreamed the housing would be so expensive."

"Oh, I have been so busy, I didn't get a chance to tell you that Dad thinks he can secure a house-sitting arrangement for you. One of his staff must go on a three-month assignment and he needs someone to house sit and keep his dog and cat from dying."

Allie was silent.

"Allie?"

"I'm, um, I am speechless. You and your dad are doing so much for me. I don't know how to thank you. I hope you can deduct me in some way on your taxes as, um, sort of a donation to a nonprofit. I don't know how to thank you."

"Well, you'll be doing this guy a favor. Dog and cat care is incredibly expensive in DC. You can save up the first and last month and deposit for your own place now."

Allie was silent.

"Allie, are you okay?"

"Um, yeah. When will you arrive for graduation?"

"I should be on the road first thing tomorrow. I have some paperwork I need to finish up here. I didn't tell you before, but on the night I returned from Berea, someone had vandalized my cottage."

"What? Why didn't you share that?" Allie exclaimed.

"Well, you were dealing with so much trauma yourself and I didn't want to add to your worry. I wasn't hurt or in any danger and I knew it would take us some time to catch the person. And we did catch the person last night and I have been up to my ears in processing all of that paperwork. But today is a clear day and I am looking forward to driving to Berea and celebrating your graduation. I can stay the night and help you pack your stuff for DC."

"That's okay. My mom and Aunt Marge can help me with all that. Listen, I've got to go."

"Wait, um, Allie, are you mad at me?"

"No, I am just really busy and still worried about the trial thing. What if I take the job and house sitting and then get derailed by the trial?"

"Allie, I can't give you any details, but I want you to know that the trial thing WILL NOT derail your life. Your life will work out. I can promise you that."

"I hope so… Anyway I have to go."

Allie and Lona hung up. Both had knots in their stomach.

* * *

Lona was driving to Berea for the graduation. *I need to be alone with Allie. I have to figure out what is wrong. Perhaps she isn't gay and she wants me to back off.* She felt sick to her stomach again. Her phone rang. "Hey, Chuck What's up?"

"Lona, where are you?"

"I'm on my way to Berea, for Allie's graduation. Why? Your voice doesn't sound good."

"RJ called and said he got a voice mail from Preston thanking him for being a loyal friend. He said Preston didn't sound like himself. Then when the police went to arrest Preston, he had fled. His father said one of his pistols is missing."

"Does he know about the clothes?"

"We think his attorney made an appointment with him so he could turn himself in and he figured it out. We are worried he might be a danger to the staff at the Park and a danger to you in particular."

"Have you called Jim to alert him?"

"Yes. He is making sure the staff and Mary are safe. He has evacuated them to town, and he is staying on the park property in case Preston shows up. He has put a closed sign at the park entrance."

"Good. Do you know what car Preston might be driving?"

"A Ford 150 truck."

"Can you text me the license plate number? I am only fifteen minutes away from the park. I just left. I am coming back."

"Lona, please be careful."

"I will."

Lona texted Allie. "An emergency has come up at the park. Nothing for you to worry about. Enjoy your graduation. I am sorry I can't be there."

As Lona neared the parking lot closest to the park entrance, she saw the signs that the park was closed and she scanned the area to see if she spotted Preston's truck. The parking lot had only a few cars left in it. Then she saw a truck partially hidden by trees. It was Preston's and was parked on an employee's only access road used to transport materials to various parts of the Park maintenance area.

She parked her car and unlocked the Glove compartment and took out her Glock 22 service pistol. She called Jim and he answered.

"Jim, I have just returned and am near Preston's truck on the access road near the maintenance shed. Where are you?"

"I am positioned where I can see anyone coming off the main trail or entering it. I didn't have time to evacuate the park, but the check-in office is closed and there is a closed sign on the entrance."

"Yes, I saw that. The staff are safely off the premises?"

"Yes."

"No sign of Preston?"

"None."

"I think I know where he might be. I think he will return to the crime scene."

"You're thinking suicide?" Jim asked.

"Yes. I will go there and see if I can pick up his trail. I'll come back if I don't see any sign of him."

"Lona. I think you should wait till we get more reinforcements. I am sure there will be police coming."

"I will be careful. I would like to prevent this if I can."

"Any chance I can just order you to stay put?" Jim asked.

Lona made some static type of noise on her phone and disconnected. She smiled to herself. *That was incredibly adolescent. But I want Jim to have plausible deniability. Good old military training.*

She got out of her Jeep and approached Preston's truck carefully. She put her hand on the hood of the truck and it was no longer warm. She looked for footprints near the drivers' door and found a print leading away from the truck. She followed it to where it intersected with the trail leading to the camp site where all of this started. She returned to her jeep and got her day pack out and started off to find Preston.

Lona took off on a controlled jog on the trail. She estimated it would be about an hour at this rate to reach the camp site. She kept her eyes on the trail occasionally seeing the distinctive footprint she had seen just outside Preston's truck. She also kept listening for sounds of anyone else on the trail. Whenever she came to any trail intersections she would pause to see if the footprints went down the other trails, but they continued towards the one campsite. *Damn, my leg is definitely hurting from this pace. I still can't do any extended running on it. But my breathing is good. I'll slow for the last quarter mile or so. I don't want him to hear me.*

As Lona got close, she went into the woods bordering the camp site. She moved silently and carefully and caught a glimpse of Preston sitting at the edge of the lake. He had a bottle of brown liquid in one hand and a pistol on the ground next to him. She got as close as she could get while still keeping at least one big tree between herself and Preston. She checked that the strap holding her gun was unhooked and that she could pull the gun out easily. She eased the Day Pack off her back and peeked around the tree. Preston was about twenty yards away.

She cleared her voice and used a relaxed tone. "Preston, I don't want to startle you. I just want you to know you are not all alone out here."

He jerked around and put his hand on the gun. He squinted his eyes. "Don't come any closer. I have a gun. Don't try and stop me."

"Okay. I won't come any closer."

"It's you, isn't it. The Indian," he said.

"Yes. The Indian, Lona. I don't want you to hurt anyone else. Including yourself."

"Yeah, well, my life is already over. I won't spend what's left of it in prison."

"Preston, I think it was an accident that Matt died. I think you were drunk and angry and ashamed of what you and Matt were doing. I think it was all confused and things got out of control, and you hit him and it was just too hard."

"He didn't deserve to die. He made the mistake of liking me." He fought back a sob. "He made the mistake of loving me. And I am such a loser."

"No, no you aren't a loser."

"My dad thinks I am. He called me a fuckin' faggot. He told me I have to leave once this is all over. He wants nothing to do with me."

"Preston, a lot of parents have trouble managing their feelings when they learn their kid may be gay. And with time they often find a better way to handle their feelings."

"Well, my dad never changes his mind about anything."

"Yeah, I've gathered that impression. Your dad can be an angry, rigid man. But that is his burden. It doesn't have to be yours."

"Shut up and let me drink. I was almost there."

"Preston, you have good in you. You left a thoughtful, caring message for RJ. He is worried about you. Nobody wants you to kill yourself."

"Poor RJ. Dad made him mess up your cabin. He felt bad about that. But Dad ends up controlling everything and everyone." He took another long drink from the bottle.

"Everyone will be better off if I just end this. I know you want me dead."

"Well, I did have some anger at you, but then I visited your town. I saw where your parents live, and I asked around about your father. I found myself realizing the difficult and hard road you have been on with your dad. I don't want you to kill yourself. I think the charges will be manslaughter and you will not spend a lot of time in prison. I think you can actually find a way to believe in yourself. I've seen others do that."

Preston chugged from the bottle. "Just a little more," he mumbled.

Lona pulled her slingshot from her back pocket and placed a good rock she had gathered in the pouch. She saw Preston lift the gun. She stepped from behind the tree and released the pouch. It hit Preston's hand holding the gun which went off, discharging into the air above his head. She had already started her sprint towards him, covering the distance quickly. Her bad leg gave out as she crashed into him and rolled him on his stomach and quickly had his hands secured behind his back with the cuffs she had secured to her belt. Preston yelled and cried and cursed her, but it was over.

* * *

As Lona led Preston back down the trail she was met by Chuck and several officers. They were sweating in their vests and carrying extra guns. She handed Preston and his gun over to them. They told him he was under arrest and recited his Miranda rights. Then they led him away. "Lona, you are limping. Are you okay?" Chuck asked.

"Yes, just an old football injury."

"Right. I did a background check. They play a lot of football in Afghanistan."

"Got any Ibuprofen on you? Wait a minute, I've got some in my backpack." She slid it off and dug out her small medical kit. Chuck offered her some water and then took her backpack on his shoulder. They walked companionably along the trail.

"Can we add attempted murder to Preston's charges?" he asked.

"Nah. He was there for suicide. He made no attempt on me. He is a very troubled young man. No new charges."

"And you just walked up to him, and he just handed you his gun?"

"Oh, I distracted him with my witty conversation and then used my persuader," she showed Chuck her slingshot. "And he rolled over for me."

"Lona, you and your grandmother. Did you sing out the clan names?"

"Oops. I forgot those," she paused. "Do you think we can keep the paperwork on this brief? I really do need to get to a graduation."

"I'll do my best."

"And I can tell Allie about the clothes and no trial?"

"Yep. No chance of that now."

CHAPTER 29

Despite Chuck's reassurances, It was after 11:00 pm when Lona knocked on Allie's door at the dormitory. The dorm was quiet at this time of the night and seemed deserted. *I wonder if everyone is out with their families or with their friends. Having a school in a dry campus certainly cuts down on the noise. I sure hope Allie is here.*

"Who is it?"

"It's me, Lona."

"What do you want?"

"Well, I have some good news. Allie, please let me in."

Allie opened the door. The room was dimly lit by the lamp on the desk, and it was packed with boxes and clothes strewn about.

"Allie, you look like you've been crying. What is going on?"

"What do you care? You weren't even here for one of the bigger days of my life."

"Please let me explain."

"I get it," Allie interrupted. "You just feel sorry for me. You have your plans, and I don't fit into them. As soon as this legal stuff is over, I won't be your burden anymore."

Lona stood in stunned silence as she closed the door behind her. Allie's back was to her. Allie was dressed in a pair of running shorts and a T-shirt. She turned around and caught Lona staring at her legs.

"What do you want and why are you staring at my legs?!"

"I want to tell you that I spent a full night searching for Preston's clothes and I found them buried in the woods, and now the police have all the evidence they need to charge him with the death of Matt. There will be no trial. And he fled to the lake today to kill himself and I was afraid he would hurt Jim or Mary looking for me, so I couldn't come to your graduation. And I did stop him from committing suicide, and I hurried here as fast as I could to give you this good news and now you are treating me like shit, and I'm staring at your legs because they are beautiful!!! And, and, I don't know why you are mad at me." Lona was out of breath and looking intently into Allie's eyes.

Allie slowly closed the distance between them, and she took Lona's face in her hands and placed her lips softly on Lona's lips. She let herself feel their softness. She shifted her head and continued to hold Lona's face while her lips met Lona's from a different angle. She felt zingers of sensation between her legs. She let her tongue make careful contact with Lona's tongue as she opened her mouth to Lona's unspoken request. Then she let her tongue go a little further into Lona's mouth and Lona latched onto the tongue and gave a low moan. Then Lona's face slipped below her hands as one leg seemed to crumble. Allie quickly caught her from falling and they both lost their balance as they fell to the bed.

"Lona, are you all right?"

"Have you never heard Joni sing about 'weak in the knees?'"

"Who? What?"

"Never mind, I am here because I love you, not because I feel sorry for you."

"Well, I love you, and when you didn't come to my graduation and you didn't talk about us being together in the future, I figured that you didn't love me. And what is going on with your leg?" Allie asked with concern on her face.

"It just got strained from having to run to the crime scene to deal with Preston. And you do make me weak in the knees. And all my plans involve the hope of being with you."

Allie squealed in delight as she moved to continue the kissing that quickly became deeper and more passionate. Both of them were pressing their bodies together. Lona couldn't help herself from lifting Allie's T-shirt up and she was delighted there was no bra to block her from Allie's soft round breasts.

Allie was struggling with her desire to be touched and by her desire to get Lona's shirt off and see her breasts. Lona started to giggle as she mumbled, "You first."

And Allie laughed back, "No, you, first."

Lona quickly removed her shirt and bra and then rolled Allie onto her back and got on top of her lying fully stretched out as she kissed Allie with deepening hunger.

Then Allie stiffened. Her breathing got shallow as she pushed Lona off her.

"I, I can't breathe. I'm, I'm sorry, I don't know what is wrong."

Lona kept her body next to Allie's side and looked at her face. "Allie, Allie, are you having a flashback?"

"What, what is a flashback?"

"That is when you and your body are not fully here in the 'here and now.' But you are somewhere in a 'then and there.' Perhaps my being on top of you triggered a flashback of when Preston was on top of you."

Allie started to cry. "Oh, Lona. I am so sorry. I hate Preston. How can he be here?! I love you. Oh, Lona, what if he broke me? What if I won't be able to, you know, to let you touch me?!!"

"Okay, Allie, we are just going to slow this down. This was my fault."

"No. You're not to blame."

"Okay. But I was not being careful enough."

"I don't want you to be careful. I was having so much pleasure. I was so turned on. It was the best touch of my life, and now…" She dissolved into more tears.

When her tears had slowed, Lona got them both some tissues from the box on the bedside table. "Okay, please, sweetie, just let your breathing deepen and know that you are safe. This is just a speed bump. You know what a speed bump is, right? They are there to slow things down, but they do not mean the road is closed."

"But how can we go down this road when you can't even lie on top of me?"

"Well, there are so many things we can do that won't trigger this feeling of panic. You were great with the kissing, and it was just being underneath my body that triggered the flashback. We will absolutely find workarounds for this."

"Lona, I, I am worried about me and sex."

"Is it the religion stuff? The Bible?"

"No, at least I don't think so."

"Well, what is it?"

Allie felt herself get hot with shame. "The night in the tent. I was dreaming that I was in a bear den and the bear pulled me to her and I was warmed by her fur and her body. And then she pulled me to her chest and then I had my mouth on her nipple. And then, dear god, I ... I was sucking it and enjoying her warm milk. And then I woke up and I was sucking on your nipple. Good god, Lona, my first sex dream ever was with a bear!!" Allie looked away filled with shame.

"Well, Allie, I am a little freaked out. NOT because you had that dream about a bear but because I think my grandmother has been very busy visiting you in your dreams and visiting me in my dreams."

"I'm confused," Allie replied. "You think I am having sex dreams about your grandmother?!"

Lona burst out laughing.

"Dammit, Lona, why are you laughing?"

Lona struggled to control her laughter. "Remember when I told you our beliefs are complicated? The bear is my grandmother's and my, um, sort of spiritual cousins. Our spirit animals. I don't know the right words. But we believe our souls try to communicate with us in dreams, and our souls communicate with other souls in dreams. And lots of times things are symbolic, not just concrete in dreams. The significant thing is that the bear was nurturing you, not having sex with you. The bear was sort of leading you to me, to my bear energy of strength and protectiveness. Our sexual feelings are what we and our body soul bring to the equation."

"Body soul?"

"Yeah, we have more than one soul, sort of each with a different job to perform."

"Do you know how strange all this sounds to me?" Allie asked softly.

"Yeah, I do. Do you know how strange it sounds to me that the Holy Spirit got Mary pregnant without sex and she then had a son who was a god and a human. And her husband, Joseph, went along with it because the spirit told him it would be okay?"

Allie smiled, "Well when you say it that way, I get why it sounds strange. Clearly, we are a species that can come up with some weird sounding explanations. But, Lona, I do believe in my religion. It is important to me to believe in the story of Jesus."

"And, Allie, it is important to me to believe in my people's story of our souls and in the communication between souls. And I am okay with us having some different explanations for how the world works. Are you?" Lona asked.

Allie took a deep breath. "Okay, as long as I don't have to have sex with bears."

Lona chuckled. "My people, historically, accepted that women sometimes took women as partners. They were viewed as warriors or two souls. I hope your beliefs can allow us to love each other."

Allie looked thoughtful. "The Jesus I believe in wanted people to be more loving. So I think he would be okay with us."

"Great. I was not expecting us to have this conversation in the middle of our first physical encounter. And I have some more spooky stuff to tell you," Lona said. "I did not find Preston's buried clothes by myself. My repetitive dreams of being in the woods and following a bear always had a fallen, moss-covered tree in them. I think my grandmother's soul helped me. There are a thousand old fallen trees in those woods. I chanted and got still like I'm supposed to, and two friggin' squirrels showed me where Preston's clothes were buried, under a specific moss-covered, fallen tree."

"Okay, you are giving me the shivers," Allie said.

"Me, too. Let me ask you this. Since the dream on the tent night, have you had other sex dreams?"

"Yes."

"All with bears?"

'Well, no, thank goodness. Dreams with some woman's body. And lately, I've been thinking of you, and I touch myself and I, um, masturbate."

"Well, there you have it, seems to me, you want to have sex with women, not bears."

"Lona, I want to have sex with you."

"Okay, let's take advantage of what you have already learned about yourself and touch. I will just support that. I absolutely know you will get past the panic your body felt with Preston."

"How do we do that?"

"Well, let me get some cream from my backpack, and let's start with the kissing again, we know we both like that. She reached over and got out the cream and put it on the nightstand. Once you are feeling nicely aroused again, I will sit back and use your headboard to support me, and you will sit between my legs with your back to me."

"And then what?"

"I won't tell you now, but how about you just shut up and kiss me?"

Allie started slowly and Lona was careful to not go any faster than Allie. In a short amount of time, Allie whispered, "I want more." And Lona sat back against the headboard, and positioned Allie to sit between her legs facing away from her.

"Can you let your breathing deepen and just lay your head back to one side of my head?" Lona softened her voice until she was whispering "I am going to touch your ear very slowly with my tongue. You can just notice the path my tongue takes on your ear." Lona felt Allie relax and heard her gasp in a delighted way.

"My other ear wants some, too."

"Allie," Lona whispered in her ear, "Can you say, 'Please'"?

"Oh, yes, Please, please."

When Lona felt Allie moving her legs with the building sensations, trying to rub herself by pressing her legs together, she reached around and started to rub the oil back and forth on Allie's breasts and nipples. "Allie, I'm thinking you would like to touch yourself now, between your legs." Allie moaned and found the spot of most pleasure, and she started a rhythm that eventually became faster and harder. And Lona matched the intensity with more pressure on her nipples. Allie reached up and grabbed Lona's hair with her other hand as she pressed her head back against Lona's neck, her body stiffened with the release that shook her from her head to her curling toes. Then she slumped and was deliciously limp as Lona rocked her slowly and whispered about her beauty…

* * *

The morning sun was bathing the room in light. Allie slowly opened her eyes and felt Lona's body spooning her. Lona's arm was draped around her waist. She carefully lifted Lona's arm off her and moved away as Lona shifted and turned to her other side, her dark hair spread out on the pillow.

Allie watched Lona breathe. *I can't believe Lona is actually in my bed. I think I could watch her sleeping every day of my life. I can't believe how much I liked us making love last night. But I wish I had been able to make love to her. I was so tired, I just sort of passed out. Man, that was some heavy sleep. Mom and Marge aren't supposed to be here for an hour. Perhaps I will just start touching her and wake her up that way. I loved that ear thing, I'm going to do that to her.*

As she leaned over Lona's ear, Lona started to mumble and

jerk her legs. And she was making noises that sounded like a strangled cry. Then Lona swung her elbow and caught Allie in the stomach.

"Ooph," Allie said as she reached over to hold Lona's arms so she couldn't hit her. "Lona, Lona, it's me, Allie. Wake up. You're having a nightmare."

"What? Who?"

"It's me, Allie. It's just a nightmare."

Lona got still. "Did I hit you?"

"Nothing major. Just a weak elbow in my stomach. You get nightmares too?"

"Not so much anymore. Perhaps it was being around a guy with a gun again that triggered this one."

"Lona, who had a gun? Preston?"

"Yes, I thought I told you he tried to commit suicide."

"I remember that, I guess I didn't know how. And then we started kissing and that pretty much pushed everything out of my mind."

"Yeah, me too. That was amazing."

"Okay, but back to Preston. Did he point the gun at you? Did he fire at you?

"No, his plan was to shoot himself, but whenever you try and stop someone from doing that, they can easily turn on you and shoot you and then themselves, or they will point the gun at you and hope you shoot them."

"Did you use your gun to make him drop his gun?" Allie asked, her eyes widening.

"No, He wasn't going to stop just because I told him to

stop. I tried that. But I had my slingshot aimed at him and I hit his hand with the stone and that threw off his aim and he dropped his gun, and then I was able to get to him before he could get his gun in his hand again."

Allie's face went white.

Lona reached for her hand. "Oops, My bad. Too much information. Really, I was never in any real danger."

"Okay," Allie said moving her hand away from Lona. "Now you are lying to me. I may be more careful in my questions in the future, but do not treat me like a child. That was terribly dangerous, and I hate thinking that you could die just from doing your job. I think I hate your job. It will take me some time to get used to the fact that you do this kind of work."

"Well, typically forest rangers have lives of just checking people in and out of the park and cleaning up campsites and leading tours and sometimes trapping hurt or nuisance skunks," Lona said in her most reassuring voice.

Allie just glared at her.

"Well, that was what I hoped for when I joined," Lona hurried to say. "But I haven't had time to tell you that I will be stopping my work with the Park Service at the end of this summer."

Allie looked closely at Lona. "But what are you going to do then?"

"I plan on going to college."

Allie held her breath, and then asked in a soft voice: "Where and to study what?"

"I want to study counseling or psychology. I want to help

people that way."

Allie leaned forward and hugged Lona and started to cry. "Oh, I am so relieved. Do you know where you want to apply to school?"

"Well, I think I will get my required courses at a junior college and then go to a four-year college and perhaps grad school. I am looking for schools in the DC area."

Allie let out a squeal. "I don't know what to say. We can be in the same town, maybe even in the same apartment! Am I getting ahead of myself here?"

"No," Lona said brushing the hair away from Allie's eyes. "I have had you in my mind as part of all of my planning."

"Why didn't you tell me before? I have been thinking I was the only one who wanted a future with you!!"

"We have both been pretty busy. And the court thing has only been finished for one day. I think I told you I couldn't risk being involved with you, you know, romantically, until that was over."

They both moved to hold each other, smiling. Soon they were kissing again. Allie pulled away. "So, you didn't get a turn last night. I want to help you have some pleasure. I want to make love to you. I want to finally get a chance to see all of your body and touch you all over," she said as she started to lift the sheet off of Lona's body.

Lona reached quickly for the sheet and held it over herself. She took a deep breath.

"Uh, oh," Allie said. "The deep breath thing again. You don't want me to touch you?"

"I feel really self-conscious about my legs," Lona said with a shaky voice.

"What? Why? Your legs are beautiful. Your entire figure is beautiful. Please, let me see your legs."

"I haven't let anyone see them since the doctors and nurses worked with them in rehab." Lona replied, still holding the sheet.

"Dammit! Rehab? Just how much do I NOT know about you?"

"An IED went off near me and my legs are quite scarred. The leg you saw me favoring was the most damaged, but, thankfully, the doctors saved it. It doesn't bother me unless I use it too much. Like in running too far."

Allie moved away from Lona. "Oh, Lona, I didn't know. And I am so sorry for what you have gone through with that. But I still want to touch you from your toes to the top of your head. Will you let me?"

A long silence ensued. Allie could see the battle going on inside of Lona. Finally, she said, "Okay." And she slowly lifted the sheet and uncovered her entire body. Lona scanned Allie's face for signs of disgust. She saw Allie tilt her head and her eyes widen. She saw Allie lean closer and inspect her legs.

"Gosh, that is a lot of scars. It is like someone took a pink magic marker and then just drew lines … like randomly on brown paper. The lines are heavier in some places and lighter in others. And then these larger patches of pink. Can you hand me the cream you used on me last night? Could I use that on your legs?" Allie asked.

"Yes. The doctors say it will help the scars stretch and fade with time. But they will never totally disappear," Lona handed the cream to Allie.

Allie took the cream and started on the foot of the leg with the most scars. She slowly rubbed the cream on Lona's foot, carefully and skillfully massaging the tendons and muscles in her arch.

"That actually feels good," Lona said.

"Right? After a cross-country meet, we usually get a good massage on our feet and legs to help with the soreness. Tell me if anything is tender or if my pressure is too much." Then Allie moved her hands over Lona's calf, spreading the cream over every inch of her leg and then up onto the muscles of her thigh.

Lona felt herself starting to relax. Allie stopped at the top of her thigh and then returned to the bottom of her leg again and then used her cheek to continue rubbing the cream into Lona's skin. She went more slowly with her cheek and when she got to the inside of Lona's thigh, she heard Lona's breathing quicken.

"Okay, the nurses and PT people never used their cheek on me, and I don't think they went that high, and I'm sure they didn't blow their warm breath on me," Lona murmured in a low voice.

"What a bunch of losers," Allie said, and they both laughed. Allie heard Lona's voice catch, and when she looked up she saw tears on Lona's cheeks. She slid her face up to Lona's and gently licked the tears off.

"Allie, I don't know what to say. I never thought anyone would ever enjoy looking at my legs again."

"Oh, I not only like looking. I like touching them. They are beautiful and strong, and they have the most interesting wrapper I have ever seen. Let me kiss you while I am up here and then I want to have an intimate meeting with your other leg."

Lona could feel the 'dam-breaking' thing happen in her chest again and she held Allie close to her and felt like she wanted to take her into her body…

There was a loud knock on the door.

CHAPTER 30

"Allie, it is your mother and Aunt Marge. We have brought some breakfast."

Both Allie and Lona jumped from the bed, throwing their clothes on. Lona used her hands to comb her hair into place. She checked that her zipper was closed and grabbed a pillow and blanket and made a hasty bed on the floor as if she had slept there. She nodded to Allie who was also dressed and who then opened the door.

"Oh, hi, Lona. I didn't know you were here. We missed you yesterday. Lona, this is my sister, Marge. I know we are a little early, I hope we didn't wake you."

"No, we were just getting up, Mom," Allie took over. "Hi, Aunt Marge."

Marge came forward and took Lona's outstretched hand in both of hers. "Thank you for all that you have done for our family."

"I feel like I know you from all that Allie has told me about you," Lona replied holding Aunt Marge's hand in hers. "Let's see if we can clear some space for you guys."

Allie's mom started to pass around the food. "I hope we have brought enough."

"Lona and I can share the coffee and breakfast sandwich," Allie said, handing the coffee cup to Lona who gratefully took a large sip.

"I am sorry I missed the graduation ceremony yesterday, but there was a big breakthrough in the case against Preston and I had to be at the park to handle that. I got in late last night so I could tell Allie the good news that new evidence was found. Now Preston is in jail, and his father was charged with vandalism of my cottage. Preston will be charged in the death of Matt. There will not be a trial and Allie will not have to testify."

"Oh, thank goodness," both women exclaimed.

Allie continued distributing the food and pulled up a box so she and Lona could sit together and let her mom and Marge take the chair and bed.

"What evidence?" Aunt Marge asked settling herself into the chair.

"Lona found the clothes Preston was wearing. He had buried them in the woods, and they had Matt's blood on them," Allie said.

Allie's mom leaned over and hugged her sister who was crying softly with this news. Allie and Lona sat silently. Eventually Allie said, "And yesterday Preston then tried to commit suicide and Lona stopped him and that is why she couldn't be here."

Both women looked at Lona, who offered, "I know this doesn't lessen the loss of Matt. But it does lessen the time of not knowing what will happen to Preston."

"Lona, the police haven't told us much about what really happened. The doctor or maybe a police officer did tell us that Matt was not alive when he was placed in the water. Can you tell us anymore? Did he suffer?" Aunt Marge asked.

"What else were you told?" Lona inquired.

"That he was killed by a single blow to his head, possibly a rock ... swung with great force. Do you think the death was instant? I want to believe that he would have helped Allie if he could have."

"From what I saw and read in the reports, it looked like the blow to his head was severe, his death was not immediate, but he may have lost consciousness. It looked like he tried to crawl to Allie, perhaps when he heard her yelling. He was able to drag himself about twenty yards towards where Preston had Allie pinned to the ground. Then he could crawl no more and he lost consciousness and bled out. He died trying to get to Allie."

All three women were silent as they digested this news. Then they each got up and stood together holding and crying together, over-flowing with the pain, pride, and relief.

Eventually Aunt Marge said, "Thank you, Lona, for telling us that. I will hold dear my son's courage."

"Yes," Allie said, "I believed Matt would have helped me if he could. Now I know for sure."

Aunt Marge continued, "Lona, there are some rumors that Matt and Preston were sexual with each other. Do you know if that is true?"

"Would that make a difference in how you feel about

Matt?" Lona asked softly.

"No. But I regret he didn't trust me enough to tell me he was gay. I would have wanted him to know that I loved him, no matter what. Actually, I wouldn't have been surprised if he told me he was gay."

"Well, I'd like to believe that he does know how much all of you loved him," Lona said.

They were all silent.

"We are all so aware now that we don't always have the time we think we have to tell each other the important things," Allie's mom said as she looked directly at Allie. "Honey, is there something you need to tell me?"

"Why? What? Umm, not sure what you mean, mom."

"Well, I think even a blind person could see that you and Lona have a special feeling for each other. And I don't think Lona slept on that hard floor," she said with a sly smile.

Allie shot a look at Lona who just took a deep breath and nodded to her. "Umm, well, I was not ready to have this conversation. Frankly, I only got aware of … of these feelings towards Lona in the last few weeks. I've been kind of closed off to any of those feelings until recently. But you're right. I am crazy about her, and we didn't do anything about these feelings until last night."

"And just so you know, Mrs. Cooper, I am in love with your daughter," Lona said taking Allie's hand in hers and facing Mrs. Cooper.

Aunt Marge went to the food bags and pulled out the orange juice and handed some to each them. "A toast to new feelings: A toast to love."

They drank and then they hugged and laughed, and all started talking at once about Allie's and Lona's plans and the move to DC.

EPILOGUE

One Year Later

Allie fumbled with her key to unlock the front door to the apartment she shared with Lona. She was balancing a brown bag with the vintage briefcase that Lona had given her for her birthday.

Finally getting the door unlocked, she called out, "Lona, are you home?"

"In here. I'm looking through the fridge to see what I can make for dinner. Did you pick up anything on your way home?" Lona replied.

"Oops. No," she said as she nuzzled Lona's neck reaching around her to place a bottle of champagne in the freezer. "Any chance you can go out and kill us a squirrel, or rabbit, or maybe that yappy little dog next door? It would go well with the champagne I brought home."

Lona turned around, placing a brief kiss on Allie's cheek. "I hardly think squirrel would go well with champagne, and certainly not dog, though I agree he continues to be a pest. But are we celebrating something?" She took Allie's briefcase from her, placing it on the floor near the kitchen counter. She placed her hands on either side of Allie's flushed face and kissed her softly on her lips. "Mmm. You always taste good."

"You always say that," Allie replied, slowly breaking the kiss to hold Lona as she examined her face. "Will tonight be sex before dinner or during dinner or after, or all three?"

"Well, all I can see for dinner tonight is fried potatoes and eggs. Certainly no hurry to get to that. But what are we celebrating?" Lona asked.

"Well, to be clear, I do like the way you make potatoes and eggs. Allie took Lona's hand and led her to the couch. "But I thought we'd celebrate a successful first year at college, and you making the Dean's list, oh, and you getting that scholarship for next year. I couldn't be more proud of you."

"Of us," Lona replied, starting to unbutton Allie's black blouse. "I couldn't have done it without your help. You make a great tutor."

"Yes, I do," Allie murmured. "I have always found having sex as a reward for completed homework helps my students stay focused and productive."

Lona continued to unbutton Allie's blouse. "Hmm, and you are wearing my favorite black bra today. I love having you come home every night in a good mood." She slipped her fingers inside Allie's bra and enjoyed her search for what lay beneath the fabric.

Allie moaned. "Jeez, I like how you say hello. If this goes any further, I may forget my good news."

Lona slowly pulled back and gazed into Allie's eyes. "Tell me, sweetie, what is your good news?"

"Well, I got a promotion, and it comes with a raise, and

they want to send me to the Navajo reservation to consult on a project this summer."

"How long would you be gone?" Lona asked softly.

"I think about a month on the project, but I also have accumulated ten days' vacation, and I thought we could both go. You know, and you could show me where you grew up, and I could meet some of your cousins and aunts…" She pulled a small box from her pocket, "And, umm, I would like for us to get married and maybe have a ceremony at your special place, at your canyon." She watched Lona's face as she digested all this information.

Lona closed her eyes and breathed deeply. "Well, yes. I absolutely want to marry you. I thought you'd never ask," she said with a wink. "And I am so touched that you would want this ceremony at my tribal home, but what of your parents and my dad?"

"I thought we could do some kind of family sort of gringo thing here and some kind of spiritual ceremony there. I don't know if marriage is, like, legal, on the reservation. And this box is empty because I thought we could design the rings together – you know, some kind of combination of our symbols."

"Yeah, like having a bear prowling around a cross?" Lona asked with a smile.

"Yeah, something like that," Allie laughed.

"Oh, honey. I am all in. I hate it that my people passed their damn Dine' Marriage Act making it illegal for us to marry on the reservation, and I think it will eventually get repealed, but we could do a small private ceremony there. I need to get on the phone with my aunts. Let me get that champaign and we can skip the gourmet meal of potatoes and eggs and start our celebration here on the couch."

"And then perhaps the bedroom?" Allie added as Lona hurried to retrieve the bottle.

"Yep, and then perhaps the dining room table," Lona called out as she returned with the bottle and glasses.

"Yep, a trifecta for tonight," Allie replied.

www.ingramcontent.com/pod-product-compliance
Lightning Source LLC
LaVergne TN
LVHW091127080826
845145LV00008B/2075

* 9 7 8 1 9 3 8 8 4 2 8 2 5 *